What if...
All the Rumors Were True

Check out all the
What if books!

What if . . . Everyone Knew Your Name
What if . . . All the Boys Wanted You
What if . . . You Broke All the Rules
What if . . . Everyone Was Doing It
What if . . . All the Rumors Were True

And coming in December 2008:
What if . . . Your Past Came Back
to Haunt You

a choose your destiny
NOVEL

What if...
All the Rumors Were True

LIZ RUCKDESCHEL AND SARA JAMES

DELACORTE PRESS

Published by Delacorte Press
an imprint of Random House Children's Books
a division of Random House, Inc.
New York

Delacorte Press and colophon are registered trademarks of
Random House, Inc.

Visit us on the Web! www.randomhouse.com/teens

Educators and librarians, for a variety of teaching tools,
visit us at www.randomhouse.com/teachers

Library of Congress Cataloging-in-Publication Data
is available upon request.

ISBN: 978-0-385-73641-1 (trade)

The text of this book is set in 12.5-point Apollo MT.

Book design by Marci Senders

Printed in the United States of America

10 9 8 7 6 5 4 3 2 1

First Edition

What if...
All the Rumors Were True

ENDLESS SUMMER

Fall has a certain appeal come the dog days of summer.

"I wonder if there's a way to make the music play backward."

Haley Miller, slumped on the couch in her father's study in a pair of cutoff overalls and a tank top, snapped her head toward her seven-year-old brother, Mitchell, who was busy fiddling with her MP3 player. "What did you just say?"

"Nothing."

"Say it again."

Mitchell didn't reply.

"Come on, Mitchie. Humor me."

"I mean, if I took your MP3 player apart and put it together backward, would it play music, you know, in reverse?"

Haley could hardly believe her ears. She was so amazed she barely noticed that her brother was about to ruin her carefully programmed listening device. "One more time, Mitchie."

"Why?"

It wasn't what Mitchell said, but how he'd said it. For the first time in over a year he'd used complete sentences and spoken in a normal, human voice. Up until that very minute Haley's brother had insisted on speaking in a robotic monotone. Just. Like. This. It had worried Haley's parents no end, and of course drove her crazy.

"Mitchell, what happened? You spoke. And not like an alien."

"Duh. Why shouldn't I?" Mitchell said. "I don't live on an asteroid."

"Dad! Mom!" Haley jumped up, grabbed Mitchell's hand and ran into the kitchen, where she found her father, Perry, and her mother, Joan, scraping corn kernels off three dozen ears. They were making creamed corn to freeze for winter. Freckles, the family's excitable dalmatian, stirred from a nap and began barking, caught up in the excitement of the moment. "Listen to Mitchell!"

"Please, Haley," Joan said. "Between all the tests,

exercises and recordings we've done with him, I can't take another sentence."

"Just listen." Haley dragged Mitchell by the hand and stood him in front of her parents. "Okay, Mitchell. Go. Talk."

Mitchell, who sometimes—make that always—seemed to enjoy bothering his big sister, just smiled and said nothing.

"Talk or I'll break both your thumbs!" Haley snapped.

"No!" Mitchell cried. "I need them for playing video games."

"Exactly." She smiled triumphantly at her parents. "Did you hear that?"

"I don't see what the big deal is," Mitchell said. "I didn't grow purple wings and fly."

Joan's mouth fell open. Perry fell to his knees and hugged his little boy. "It's true!"

"Oh, thank God," Joan said. "Just in time for second grade, when the teachers don't take to eccentricities quite so kindly."

"What happened, Mitchell?" Perry asked, tousling Mitchell's hair. "Who deprogrammed you?"

"Yeah," Haley said. "It must have been hard to keep that robot gag up for a whole year."

For much of that time, Haley's parents had been dragging Mitchell from expert to expert, trying to understand their son's quirky stutter. Psychologist after psychiatrist after speech therapist had tested

Mitchell and declared, much to Joan and Perry's dismay, that the robot voice was probably just a phase. "Just a phase?" Joan kept uttering. "His imaginary friend, Marcus—that was a phase. The only-eating-brown-foods bit one winter—a pretty time-consuming but ultimately harmless phase. But this? I've never seen anything like it. And I've read all the textbooks."

Since no one seemed to be able to help little Mitchell, the Millers finally just decided to let it go for a while and see if, in fact, he would outgrow his strange and annoying speech patterns. And, much to everyone's relief, it looked as if he finally had.

"This is quite a milestone," Perry said as he jumped to his feet and left the room, returning a few seconds later with his camcorder. As a documentary filmmaker, he liked to record every event in the life of the Miller family, no matter how tedious or embarrassing.

"Are you going to make a movie about me?" Mitchell asked, looking into the camera.

"Do you want me to?" Perry asked. "I could make you my freshman class project," he teased. After taking the summer off, Perry was about to return to his job as an adjunct professor at Columbia's film school.

"What do you think is my best angle?" Mitchell asked, suddenly posing like a Mexican wrestler. "Look, Dad, I'm like one of your trees," he added, holding his arms up like branches and swaying to a make-believe breeze. Perry's most recent documentary was on the life cycle of deciduous trees.

"You're certainly a natural," Perry replied, chuckling from behind the camera as he captured Mitchell's performance.

Haley thought she still heard a slight jerkiness in her brother's speech occasionally, but whatever—this was a huge improvement. "Thanks, Mitchie."

"For what?" he asked.

"You've already improved all our lives a gazillion times over. You have no idea how annoying it was listening to you at the dinner table night after night."

"I'm glad I could be of assistance," Mitchell said, and bowed. With that, he snatched Haley's MP3 player from where he'd left it on the counter and ran out of the room.

"Oh, Mitchell," Haley called after him. "If you try to take that thing apart, I really will break your thumbs."

Haley doubted her brother would listen, but unfortunately she was too sweltering hot to chase after him. The Millers didn't believe in air-conditioning, or as Joan called it, "That carbon-hogging contraption that anesthetizes you from feeling the effects of climate change." Summer was dragging on into its last days, and the muggy New Jersey weather had Haley's brain in a fog. For starters, she could hardly believe she was about to enter the junior class at Hillsdale High. This time last year, when the Miller family was in the process of moving cross-country from Northern California, her future had seemed completely open. Unknowable. A blank slate.

But now everything was different. Haley knew who her friends were. Or at least she thought she did. She understood the lay of the land at her new school, Hillsdale High, and she only very rarely got lost in the maze that was the math wing these days. And yet, a lot of loose ends had been left hanging when she finished up her sophomore year and plunged into summer. With school about to start in just a few days' time, Haley was once again unsure of where she stood in the Hillsdale hierarchy.

Everything and everyone had changed so much in the past year. When she came to Hillsdale, Coco De Clerq, Whitney Klein and Sasha Lewis were the social queen bees who lorded it over the class and much of the rest of the school. Now Coco was obsessed with the gubernatorial campaign of Eleanor Eton, the mother of her boyfriend, Spencer. Perpetual beta girl and Coco-sidekick Whitney was coming into her own as a local fashion designer, and Sasha had abandoned the populette life for soccer and rock 'n' roll.

At the other end of the spectrum, supernerds Annie Armstrong and Dave Metzger had gone to Spain over spring break and returned a couple—the trip abroad had completely transformed the book-worms into Latin lovers. But after a brief flirtation with bohemian rhapsody, they were inching back to their old grade-grubbing selves. The two had spent the summer in a kind of academic cyberspace. Dave went to computer camp in Washington, D.C., learning videocasting, while Annie studied creative writing and grammar—of course, how could she leave out grammar?—at a workshop in upstate New York. The college race was getting serious, and Annie and Dave were not about to let any opportunities slip through their fingers. At least they were dressing slightly better and were way less uptight nowadays.

As for the artsy rebel crowd, Irene Chen, Shaun Willkommen and Devon McKnight were mellowing in their antisociety stance. Shaun had even taken up track and field the previous spring. Haley never thought she'd see pudgy Shaun voluntarily participating in a sport, but she suspected that part of the attraction was the clothes. Shaun had bought seventies track suits from Jack's, the vintage clothing store where Devon worked after school. He accessorized the outfits with capes and headbands and gold lamé, making him look like Hillsdale's own Evel Knievel. That comparison was actually not so far off base, since Shaun had, after all, launched himself through a flaming heart on Valentine's Day to prove his love for Irene.

On the other hand, thanks to all the shenanigans, the rebels had done so poorly in their classes (apart from Mr. Von's art seminar) that they'd all had to go to summer school. Haley shuddered at the thought of weeks alone in a classroom with Principal Crum. Absolute hell on earth.

Then there was Reese Highland, the boy next door, who was really more like the Greek god next door. Reese was just home from this summer's tour of athletic camps, and Haley could once again see him from her window, shooting hoops in his driveway. Shirtless. She could also sometimes see him shirtless upstairs in his bedroom, which was directly across from hers. That was one good thing about the heat, at least. It meant wearing a lot fewer clothes. Reese was all-star material. He aced every sport he played, from soccer to basketball to track, and he was brilliant too. By all accounts, the perfect guy. But was he the perfect guy for Haley? And how would she ever know for sure? With Reese away for so much of July and August, they'd had a hard time keeping in touch. A few postcards had flown back and forth, and there had been that hasty phone call over the Fourth of July. But now, Haley wasn't sure if they were friends, boyfriend and girlfriend, or just neighbors with a little history who happened to be in the same class.

Haley didn't know who she was going to be this year, but she did know one thing: whoever she was, she needed a new pair of jeans, something that would make just the right statement on her first day back on campus.

"Mom, I think it's time for some back-to-school

shopping," Haley announced, snapping out of her daze and looking disapprovingly down at her cutoff overalls.

"Ooh, ooh, ooh, me too," Mitchell said, racing back into the kitchen. "I need some fancy second-grade clothes. Sports jackets, ties, stuff like that."

"Well, I don't know about sports jackets . . . ," Joan said. "But I guess we can go to the . . . the . . . mall." Joan shivered, her eyes filling with terror. Haley's mother had an almost physical intolerance for shopping of any sort. Well, of any sort that didn't involve young tomato plants, gardening tools, compost bins or bean sprouts.

"Does Mitchell have to come?" Haley complained.

"Sorry, honey, I don't have time for two trips," Joan said. Actually, the look on Haley's mother's face made it clear she would likely have trouble getting through just one.

Haley left Mitchell and Joan in the boys' department at the anchoring department store, and went in search of jeans she wouldn't be mortified wearing. As she stepped off the escalator in the mall's main pavilion, she nearly ran smack into bubbly, blond Whitney Klein, who was loaded down with shopping bags.

"Haley!" Whitney air-kissed each of Haley's

cheeks. "Finally losing those California hippie over-alls once and for all?" Whitney added, giving Haley's denim a dismissive glance.

"Uh, I guess," Haley said, feeling self-conscious as she eyed Whitney's shopping bags. Haley hoped Whitney had paid for all that stuff. Whitney, as everyone in Hillsdale well knew, had developed something of a shoplifting habit the previous school year, and Haley had never quite figured out whether she had really gotten over the obsession.

"I'm stealing—I mean borrowing—ideas for next season. Never too early to start sketching the spring line! Don't worry, I paid for everything," Whitney clarified.

"That's great," Haley said, relieved to know that a dozen mall cops weren't about to descend on them, Tasers drawn.

"You know, copper's really in this fall." Whitney reached into a bag and flashed the toe of a new pair of metallic copper-colored boots. "It's this season's lime green." Everyone had been sporting the neon shade all summer in Hillsdale. "You should really get a copper-colored bag, Haley. It would look awesome with your hair!"

Haley tugged at a strand of her long auburn mane. She'd been thinking of getting a new bag, and Whitney's color selection was actually not half bad. "Maybe," Haley said.

"Hey, did you hear about Zoe Jones?" Whitney

suddenly asked, leaning close to Haley and dropping her flighty voice to what was internationally known among sixteen-year-old girls as gossiptone.

"No," Haley said. She'd been pretty out of the loop on rumors all summer.

"I heard that she became a total groupie with that new band Motormouth from Saddle River," Whitney said. Haley had actually heard of Motormouth, at least. Anyone within listening distance of an SUV with booming bass speakers that summer probably had. The rising New Jersey rap-rock group, led by a charismatic singer named Pi-Rex, had seemingly captivated every DJ in the tristate area.

Motormouth would make a great nickname for Whitney, Haley thought, watching her classmate babble on.

"It doesn't seem like such a big deal," Haley said. "Zoe's a musician. She probably just wants to learn the business from professionals."

"Yuhright," Whitney scoffed.

Dark, beautiful Zoe Jones had been voted Most Talented, Best All-Around and Most Likely to Be Famous in last year's freshman class, making her a clear and present danger to her older female peers. Whitney was just one of the girls who felt threatened. Zoe was also the current star of the local new-wave pop group Rubber Dynamite, which had won the Hillsdale-Ridgewood Battle of the Bands contest in the spring, mostly on the strength of Zoe's musical talent, beauty and stage prowess. Just another reason for Whitney to fear and revile her.

"Does learning the business involve throwing yourself at Pi-Rex, and offering to do anything, and I mean anything, to go on tour with them?" Whitney asked, her face growing flushed at the thought of the *scandale*.

"Maybe she meant 'anything' like loading amps and setting up mikes," Haley suggested.

"Well, I heard she did everything but," Whitney said. "With all of them. That's pretty slutty for a girl who isn't even a sophomore yet."

Haley was skeptical. She didn't know Zoe all that well, but then, neither did Whitney. "Where did you hear this?" Haley demanded.

"Oh, come on, Miller. Everybody knows about it," Whitney said. "So it must be true. Now. I've got to run, but I'll see you at school. Oh, and at SAT prep. You're going, right? Big kiss!"

"Right," Haley said, her mind wandering as Whitney teetered away in her summery high-heeled lime green espadrilles.

SAT prep. Haley vaguely remembered that her mother had mentioned something about signing her up for that. The conversation had taken place on a particularly sweltering day, when the thermometer had topped out at 105 degrees and Haley had vegetated in an almost catatonic state in front of the fan in her room. No wonder it hadn't really registered.

Haley wandered into the teen department and picked out the most neutral pair of jeans she could find—higher-waisted than the lowriders she already owned, which sometimes exposed her underwear and infuriated her parents, but not crazy-high, like mom jeans. The leg was a little fuller than her stovepipes, but not bootcut. . . . It was a very delicate balancing act, finding just the right pair to go anywhere at any time.

Haley caught up with her mother and little brother at the checkout counter.

"I bought a bow tie," Mitchell announced, showing off his red plaid Young Republican neckwear.

"Great, Mitch," Haley said, practically ignoring him.

Joan sighed. "As if coming to the mall weren't bad enough, he insisted on shopping the country club aisles. Welcome to Mitchell's latest phase. Now that he's not a robot anymore, he's turning into Merv Griffin."

"Who's Merv Griffin?" Haley asked, completely lost.

"Only the greatest entertainer who ever lived," Mitchell interjected, putting on his new bow tie over his T-shirt.

Joan rolled her eyes. "He was an old talk-show host. What do you kids say we stop off at Golden Dynasty on the way home and pick up some Chinese takeout for dinner?"

"Fine with me," Haley said. Irene Chen's parents owned the Golden Dynasty, and Irene sometimes worked there. It might be interesting to see who else was hanging around. Like, say, her friend the adorable photographer Devon McKnight.

Joan called in the order on her cell as they carried their bags through the parking lot to their hybrid SUV. Ten minutes later, they were pulling up in front of the Golden Dynasty. Joan handed Haley some cash, and Haley climbed out of the car and walked under the gold-painted dragon that arched over the entrance to the restaurant. Just as she had hoped, Irene was working the hostess station, but there was no sign of Devon or, for that matter, Irene's boyfriend, Shaun.

Irene's jet-black hair was streaked with blue, braided and knotted Princess Leia–style on top of her head. She had a rather large white peony tucked behind one ear, and she wore a white vintage house-dress with a red vinyl belt. Her striped black and white leggings led down to gold vintage pumps. "Hey, Haley. I believe this is yours?" Irene handed Haley a large heavy bag that smelled not unpleasantly of hoisin sauce. "Tell your dad I put extra MSG in there just for him."

"Thanks," Haley said, smiling knowingly. She could not get over how girly Irene looked. Getting a boyfriend was having a miraculous effect on her friend's wardrobe. "So, what's new since I saw you last?"

Irene shrugged and indicated the restaurant around her. "Do you see anything new around here?"

"I know the feeling," said Haley, reflecting on her own less-than-exciting summer.

"Of course, anything's better than school," Irene said. "This year's going to suck worse than usual, too. My father and Shaun's dad have teamed up to get us a tutor. So on top of going to school all day five days a week, I've got to get schooled after school. All because my dad thinks I'll never get into any college if I don't get my GPA up."

At that moment, Irene's father smiled from the back of the restaurant, waved, pointed to the new Harvard sweatshirt he was wearing, then motioned toward Irene.

"Clearly, he's crazy if he thinks I'm getting in there," Irene said, swirling her finger in the air next to her head.

Haley smiled and waved back to Mr. Chen.

"I think it's sweet he's being so supportive," said Haley.

"Whatever. At least he's gotten used to the idea of me spending time with Shaun. Of course, he's insisting Devon join us on the tutoring sessions. And anyone else we can find. He doesn't like the idea of Shaun and me spending so much 'semi-alone' time together. As if a group would stop us from making out. So, what do you say, you want in?"

"Huh?" Haley asked.

"On our tutoring group," Irene repeated. "Look, Miller, I know you're a genius and all, but it's free help on your homework. Even Annie Armstrong would accept an offer like that."

"I'll have to think about it," Haley said, paying for the food. "See you Monday." She grabbed the bag and hurried out to the waiting SUV as Irene took out a manicure kit and began filing her nails.

"How's Irene?" Joan asked as Haley climbed into the car and slammed the door.

"The universe is totally off-kilter."

"What do you mean?" Joan asked.

"Well, Irene's gone glam, and she's . . . getting a tutor," Haley said, still perplexed at the thought of her friend actually studying. "She asked me if I wanted to join her. I mean them. Shaun's doing the tutoring sessions too."

"What about De-von?" Mitchell asked, making kissy faces in Haley's direction. "Are you two gonna quiz each other? What happens if you get one right?"

"Shut up, twerp," said Haley, shoving Mitchell against the backseat. "I think I liked you better as a robot."

"That won't work with your SAT prep class," Joan noted. "There isn't time after school for both and everything else you've got going on. And Barbara Highland thinks it's important for you kids to get in some practice work for these tests. They can be very stressful, from what I hear, and even bright kids like you and Reese can use a little help and reassurance now and then." Barbara was Reese's mother; that probably meant Haley's hot neighbor was in the class. "It's your decision," Joan added, pulling out of the Dynasty's long driveway. "But I really think SAT prep is the way to go."

Haley thought of Reese, and then of Devon, and she wasn't entirely sure she agreed.

● ● ●

It's back-to-school time, and that means back to social cliques, back to gossip and, unfortunately, back to studying. Haley's already got a lot on her plate for her busy junior year. As an upperclassman, she'll have more fun—and more responsibility. But those underclassmen are catching up fast. Could the talk about Zoe Jones possibly be true? Haley has no idea, but she does have a sinking feeling she'll be hearing an awful lot about Zoe this year.

In the meantime, Haley's got to buckle down and get ready for college. Almost everyone in her class—and that means studious Annie and Dave, Sasha, Cecily, Reese and even Coco De Clerq and Whitney Klein—will be taking the same SAT prep course. Not a surprise, really, since the Hillsdale *Sentinel* claimed "the course is guaranteed to deliver the highest possible SAT scores," and what Hillsdale parent could resist that promise? Haley knows she could use the help, but on the other hand, a lot of counselors emphasize grade point averages over SATs. Maybe small-group tutoring would actually help her more?

Haley's decision is in your hands. If you think she should follow the crowd—and Reese Highland—to SAT prep, turn to page 19 (SAT PREP). If, on the other hand, you think Haley should worry more about boosting her GPA—and spending quality time with Devon McKnight—turn to page 32 (MEET THE TUTOR).

Will Haley reach for the Ivies, settle for a safety school or blow off college altogether when the time comes? And for now, will she spend her free periods hitting the books, loading up on extracurricular activities or joyriding through Hillsdale with all the newly licensed drivers in her class? And which boy will she choose to ride with? Hot neighbor Reese? Brooding photographer Devon? Or will a new boy enter the scene . . . ?

For junior year, every decision counts double—particularly every mistake. Rumors will fly about everyone, including Haley Miller. What if . . . they're all true?

There are people who test well naturally, and then there are people who work the system.

"The college admissions game is tougher than ever, Snoodles," Perry Miller said as he steered the hybrid SUV into a strip-mall parking lot in downtown Hillsdale. "I see it at Columbia every day. Your mom and I just want you to have your best shot at getting into whatever school you decide you want to attend. I know it's stressful, but the key is to focus on your strengths, and, uh, strengthen them. Even more."

"Okay," Haley said skeptically. The problem was, she wasn't sure what her strengths were, exactly. She was smart, but did she have the academic drive of, say, Annie Armstrong? Haley was athletic, but was she soccer-scholarship material? And what about all her other interests? Which one would help her get into her dream school? And for that matter, what was her dream school? "It's all kind of overwhelming," Haley confessed, looking over at her dad.

"That's why boosting your SAT score is such a good idea." Perry pulled up in front of a storefront with an SAT PREP sign taped on the plate-glass window. A banner splayed across the brick facade promised THE BEST COURSE AROUND–GARUNTEED!!!

"Huh," Haley said. "They misspelled *guaranteed*. That's not a good sign. How much did you and Mom fork over for this?"

"I'm sure it's just a misprint," Perry said, though he looked a little alarmed. "All their ads seemed legit. And Barbara Highland told me these people got Richie Huber's brother into Dartmouth."

"Well, if Richie's brother is anything like him, that's a small miracle," Haley said as she got out of the car, relieved she wasn't a sixth-year senior. The term *stalled adolescence* had been invented for people like Richie Huber. He'd be lucky if he graduated from high school before age twenty-five.

Haley sauntered through the glass door wearing her new jeans and a pale blue and white chiffon top, her hair pinned away from her face with barrettes. She caught a glimpse of her pretty reflection in the window and liked what she saw. Haley's curves had continued to mature over the summer, and her shape was now approaching knockout status. Confidence bolstered, Haley marched up to the receptionist to check in before claiming the only free desk she saw amid a sea of familiar faces. This place might as well have been called the Hillsdale High Annex, Haley noted. Only a few Ridgewood students were sprinkled throughout the crowd. The rest of the eager test takers were Haley's classmates.

Seated on either side of Haley were Sasha Lewis and Annie Armstrong—but it was the desk behind her that Haley was most interested in. That seat belonged to Reese Highland, who took immediate notice as Haley approached. She did her best to ignore him. She was, after all, here to study. And Reese hadn't exactly been attentive for the past three months.

"Hey, Red," Reese leaned forward and whispered, his breath warm on Haley's neck. "How was your summer?"

"Not bad," Haley said cryptically. *He's not going to get off that easily,* she thought, taking out a yellow legal pad and two perfectly sharpened number-two pencils, and waited for the lesson to begin.

Dave Metzger sat on Annie's right, nuzzling Annie's hand. Beside him, the tiny savant Hannah Moss buried her head in a math book. On the other side of Sasha, the whole sweater-knotted-over-the-shoulders set—Coco De Clerq, Whitney Klein, Spencer Eton, Cecily Watson and Drew Napolitano—sat in an insular cluster. Haley had heard most of the beautiful people were trying out for the upcoming Hillsdale High production of *A Midsummer Night's Dream*—anything to pump up their transcripts with extracurriculars. On top of that, Coco and Spencer were busily campaigning for Spencer's mother, who was running for governor. Haley checked the room once more and couldn't help but notice that the only person missing from the SAT prep roster was the handsome Spanish exchange student, Sebastian Bodega.

"You wouldn't happen to be looking for Mr. Bodega, would you?" Annie asked as if reading Haley's mind. "I heard he went back to Spain over the summer for good. He's apparently engaged to that model Mia Delgado."

Haley's eyes grew as wide as saucers. Was this bit of gossip for real?

"That's not it at all," Dave whispered. "I heard Sebastian got recruited by an Olympic coach, and that he's training down in Florida. Been there since July."

That would make sense, Haley thought. Sebastian had already broken all sorts of high school records.

Hannah leaned across Dave's desk. "You're both wrong. Well, sort of. Sebastian is coming back this year."

Haley smiled.

Then Hannah added, "And so is Mia."

"What?" Annie, Dave and Haley exclaimed simultaneously.

"I helped out with paperwork in Principal Crum's office over the summer," Hannah explained. "It was the only way I could get a key to the library. Anyway, last week, I saw a folder for Mia among the stack of files for new students. Sebastian was in Miami training all summer, but Mia was there with him."

Haley gulped. Mia Delgado was about the most gorgeous thing to come out of Spain since, well, Sebastian Bodega. She had a modeling contract in New York, and Haley had even spotted her in several fashion-magazine spreads. With that girl on campus, even the stunning Sasha Lewis would look plain. What would that mean for Haley?

"Hey, Miller," Sasha said brightly. The all-American beauty was wearing green soccer shorts and a yellow tank top, her long blond hair pulled into a ponytail. "Do you have a date later or something?" she teased Haley, sizing up her swank outfit. "It's too bad you didn't come in sweats. You could have run home with me and Reese after class. Soccer starts next week, you know." Haley glanced over her shoulder at Reese, and saw that he too was in his running gear.

Shoot! Haley thought, regretting the missed opportunity, and thinking ahead to tryouts and practice and just who would captain the boys' and girls' soccer teams this year.

"So how was summer?" Sasha asked.

"Not bad," Haley said. "But then, not great either. I can't believe how little there is to do in this town."

"Why do you think I took up guitar?" Sasha replied, then expounded on the many songs she had written over break. Sasha had briefly been a member of her boyfriend's band, the Hedon, back in the spring. But the two had quickly decided it was much better to be lifemates than bandmates. Haley wondered why Sasha wasn't mentioning said boyfriend, Johnny Lane. Haley'd heard that Sasha and Johnny had gone camping together in Virginia over the summer. So why didn't Sasha mention the trip now? Was everything okay between Sasha and Johnny? Their relationship had always been a little rocky. Haley was curious to know their current status. She would have asked, but somehow SAT prep didn't seem like the right time or place.

"Hey, did you hear about Zoe Jones?" Annie suddenly whispered. Her braids dangled over Haley's desk.

"Of course," said Haley. "Who hasn't heard that one? Doesn't mean it's true."

Sasha scowled. "Ugh, I'm so sick of that rumor."

Haley wondered if Sasha wasn't just sick of hearing about Zoe Jones. Zoe's band, Rubber Dynamite, had annihilated the Hedon at the Battle of the Bands last spring. Sasha, who'd been trying to juggle track and Hedon practice all semester, had choked and forgotten the lyrics to the Hedon's one big song. It was a humiliating experience. And after a blowout with Johnny, Sasha had dropped out of the band to go solo as a singer-songwriter and to concentrate on her sports. All had ended well, but Haley wouldn't have been surprised if the whole subject was still a bit touchy for Sasha.

At that moment, the SAT prep teacher finally waltzed in, a small, thinly bearded and bespectacled young man who looked barely a year out of college. He wore a checkered cotton shirt, jeans and black high-top sneakers. "Good afternoon, young minds," he bellowed before writing his name on a chalkboard on wheels. "I'm Doug Hausner. And welcome to the most important chapter of your life to date. Statistics tell us that the college you attend will more than likely determine the jobs you will take, the cities in which you will live, the men or women you will marry. And your test scores, of course, will determine your college."

Annie was practically bouncing out of her desk with excitement. "I'm *so* focusing on school this year," she whispered to Haley. "After the debacle at the end of last year, I can't afford another slipup like that. Right, Dave?" She turned to Dave and smiled.

He beamed back at her and then grabbed her forearm and began kissing it again.

"High school determined the man you're going to marry," Dave growled, devouring Annie's flesh.

"No distractions," Annie said firmly, retrieving her limb and focusing her attention on Mr. Hausner, while Dave pouted momentarily before taking out his books.

Good to have the old Annie back, Haley thought. When Haley had first met Annie, she thought she was wound a little too tight. Okay, Haley thought Annie was like one of those accordion snakes in a can, so compressed and coiled in on itself that it was just waiting to burst. But last spring, Annie and Dave had uncoiled each other. Maybe a little too much. They had blown off their yearbook-editing responsibilities in favor of making out and slacking off, and, in the process, they had nearly kept the Hillsdale High students from having a *Talon*. Not to mention the damage they had almost done to their impeccable GPAs. Since then, Haley had revised her earlier assessment. It was just in Annie's nature to be pent up and on edge. Who was Haley to try and change her? In Annie's natural state, she was capable of almost anything. Haley wouldn't be surprised if one day Annie went on to be president or cure cancer or achieve peace in the Middle East.

"Don't get me wrong, I'm going to leave time for a

little fun, too," Annie said. "College admissions officers want to see personality. Anyone can read *Beowulf* in Old English, but can anyone say they've rewritten Chaucer as a show tune? I don't think so. Speaking of fun, I'm trying out for the debate team next week. You should try out too, Haley. College admissions officers love debaters."

Of course Annie's idea of fun would be to join the debate team, Haley thought with a smile. But she was right about one thing—debating did look impressive on a college résumé. And it was also probably a useful skill to learn. Imagine the arguments one could win against parents.

Mr. Hausner faced the class and rubbed his hands together. "Okay, kids, let's get started." It was sort of laughable the way he called everyone kids, when he was only a few years older himself. Nevertheless, the students quieted down. "As I said, my name is Doug Hausner." He pointed to each part of his name on the board as he said it, as if they couldn't read. "I'm your prep coach. So, um, let's see. Why don't we start with some questions. Yes, the girl with the braids." He called on Annie.

"What did you get on your SATs?" Annie asked boldly.

Mr. Hausner stuffed his hands in his pockets, seemingly unsure of how to respond. "Well, that's not really the point here—"

"I think it is," Annie said. "After all, our parents are paying a lot of money for this course. We should know what kind of teacher we're getting."

"You're getting the best teacher around— G-A-R-U-N-T-E-E-D!" Mr. Hausner smiled as if he expected them all to laugh at his sort-of joke, but no one did.

"Tough crowd. Moving on. So, do you all have the practice test books?"

As Mr. Hausner passed books and handouts to the class, Haley realized that he hadn't even come close to answering Annie's question. Not only did they not know his scores, they also didn't know what college he attended, or whether he'd even gone to college. *Could this place be some kind of scam?* she wondered. *Eh, who cares, as long as Reese is here.* She could feel him staring at the back of her head.

"So, let's learn how to take a test, people. What do you say?" asked Mr. Hausner. "Step one: sit at a desk. Step two: pick up a number-two pencil. Step three: take a deep breath. . . ."

Haley found herself daydreaming of Reese. His hair had gotten longer over the summer—his mother would probably say that he needed a haircut, but Haley admired the way the black tendrils curled above the collar of his bright blue T-shirt. She didn't need to be staring at that gorgeous face to see it— the sparkling eyes, the aquiline nose, the full set of lips that curled into a mischievous and irresistible smile . . . Reese Highland was, quite simply, to die for.

Concentrate, Haley, she scolded herself, snapping out of it. This was her future at stake here. And besides, Reese wasn't going to win her all over again that easily.

"So open your books and let's try the first math practice test," Mr. Hausner said. "I'll time you. You have fifteen minutes. Ready? Go."

The room fell quiet, except for the sound of scratching pencils. Haley worked the math problems as quickly as she could, filling in the appropriate A-B-C-D-E bubbles on the standardized test sheet. An hour later, Mr. Hausner went over the answers with the class. Haley was surprised to see she'd gotten all but one of the problems right. She'd done even better than Annie and Dave. She'd never really thought of herself as a math whiz but . . . who knew?

Reese tapped Haley's shoulder and, when she turned around, grinned that melting smile at her. "How'd you do?"

"Eleven out of twelve," Haley said. "How about you?"

He just grinned wider, but Haley looked down at his desk and saw that he'd gotten twelve out of twelve. "Eleven's a good score," he taunted. "Have you ever thought about joining the calculus team? We could use another brain like you for the Math Olympics."

"The math team?" Frankly, the thought had never entered Haley's mind. Maybe this was the way to solve for the square root of Reese.

"I'll think about it," she said, collecting her things. "Oh, and don't let Sasha outrun you on the way home," she added, jesting with him.

"Ha!" Reese laughed at the idea.

"I don't know, Highland. If you ask me, the summer made you soft." And with that, she strutted outside to meet her father in the parking lot.

● ● ●

Ah, another diary-worthy moment with the infamous Reese Highland. He and Haley are like Hepburn and Tracy, Bogey and Bacall, Brad and Angie. But even though Reese might be right for Haley, is he necessarily the best thing for her? If Haley falls for Reese all over again, will he support her and encourage her in her schoolwork? Or overshadow her and distract her from her goals? And where will she rank in his life? Above or below soccer, track, math club and basketball?

Decisions, decisions! It's not always easy being a well-rounded girl like Haley. She has a lot of options in front of her, and her academic—and social—future rides on the choices you make for her now. If you think the debate team is the road to college bliss, have her join Annie on page 42 (UP FOR DEBATE). To have Haley make her theatrical debut, turn to page 64 (TOTAL DRAMA). If you think Haley should put herself in the running for an athletic scholarship down the line, send her to soccer practice with Sasha on page 57 (FOR KICKS). Alternatively, you can get a behind-the-scenes glimpse at Mrs. Eton's campaign for governor in FIRST LADIES on page 72. Finally, if you think she should follow her heart and her brain to the math wing to see what Reese is up to after school these days, go to page 51 (MATH OLYMPICS).

The seeds of tomorrow are planted today. So, what's going to sprout up in Haley's next crop?

**There are some things
you just can't teach, and others
you don't want to learn.**

"Welcome to the Willkommen abode." Shaun stood at the heavy reclaimed-wood door to his family's surprisingly sleek and modern house—surprising because Shaun himself was neither sleek nor modern—while Haley, Irene and Devon dragged themselves up the steps and inside for their first tutoring session. "I welcome you on this glorious afternoon, which would more pleasantly be spent taking welcome shelter under the welcoming oaks on the lawn. *Welcome* is our word of the day. And we

Willkommens are nothing if not welcoming." He added under his breath, "Now, will someone please put me out of my misery?"

"I know, babe," Irene said, as Shaun licked her cheek hello. "I can't believe school just ended for the day and now here we are . . . back for more."

"And after a whole summer full of summer school," Devon complained. "It's like I'm stuck in—"

"A never-ending math equation?" Irene suggested.

Shaun had a devilish look in his eye. "The universe works on a math equation that never even ever really even ends in the end," he belted out, duplicating the staccato highs and lows of the Modest Mouse ditty.

"Yeah, and worse, we're high school students," snarked Irene. "And that means we're still under legal obligation to do whatever the heck our parents tell us."

"Only two more years to go, though," Devon said, his eyes looking far away at the freedoms that were yet to come.

"I know it sucks now," Shaun said. "But this tutoring crap will be worth it if it keeps me from ever having to go to HOE again. EOH morf em evaS." Haley glanced at Irene for instant translation.

"Save me from HOE," Irene said. HOE, as in "Hell on Earth," was Shaun's chosen name for summer school. Shaun had the unique ability to be able to read sentences in reverse. After years of friendship and a few months of dating, Irene was miraculously able to understand him.

It wasn't that they weren't smart, the three of them. Irene and Devon were among the brightest students at Hillsdale High, albeit in the artistic, unconventional sense. (With Shaun it was kind of hard to tell, but he did have that freakish backward-talking thing going for him.) But last spring they'd spent so much time cutting class, goofing off and just generally "enjoying life" that they'd all been ordered to go to summer school or repeat their sophomore year. And now, to prevent history from repeating itself next summer, and also because of the added pressure of junior-year transcripts, the most important grades in the most important year as far as college admissions committees were concerned, the Chens and the Willkommens had teamed up to pay for a private tutor for the artsy delinquents. Shaun's cousin, one Xavier Willkommen, was hired for the job.

"It won't be so bad," Shaun said. "Xav's pretty cool, once you get used to his—what does my dad call them?—his quirks."

"A quirky member of the Willkommen brood?" Irene asked. "You don't say."

"You'll see," Shaun said. "He goes to Tisch School of the Arts for acting. He's a theth-pian." As he said the word *thespian,* Shaun pranced around on his tiptoes, flapping his hands at the wrists. He was pretty graceful for a still slightly chubby guy. "He should be here any sec. Till he gets here, who's up for banana cheese melts? With anchovies?"

Haley, Irene and Devon exchanged glances but said nothing.

"No takers, huh?" Shaun said. "All the more for me."

"Do you have any yogurt? And maybe some granola?" Haley asked. She was a little hungry after a long day of school—just not hungry enough to stomach one of Shaun's specialty sandwiches.

"That depends. Do you take your granola with marshmallows and wasabi peas in it?" Shaun asked.

"Uh, no thanks," said Haley.

"Well, I think we gots some vanilla yogurty-goop in the fridge," Shaun said, leading them all into the kitchen. "Mom keeps all kind of weird stuff in there." Haley sorted through the entirely unweird refrigerator, locating some plain sliced cheddar cheese. "Hey, catch," Shaun said, throwing a green apple, hard, in Haley's direction. She turned just in time to instinctively raise her arms up and catch it. "She's an athlete," Shaun said as the doorbell rang. A few minutes later, an extremely tall, extremely thin young man in his early twenties strode with much affectation into the kitchen, looking as if he expected everyone to burst into applause at the sight of him. "Ladies and Devster, I give you . . . our tutor, Xavier," Shaun announced.

"Delightful to meet you ALL," Xavier said. His

wispy blond hair was cropped into a bob at his pointy chin, and he had a long, dramatic nose, the tip of which bent down and nearly met his slender upper lip. Xavier wore a billowing white shirt tucked into narrow black jeans, which in turn were tucked into his black Beatle boots. "Thhall we RETIRE to the thtudy?"

He turned and glided out of the kitchen, assuming his pupils would follow him. Irene looked at Haley. "Did he jutht thay 'thtudy'?"

Haley shrugged. "Maybe hith tongue thlipped." They followed, curious, and settled themselves at a round table near a set of floor-to-ceiling bookcases. "Now, Thhaun, who ARE your friendth?" Xavier commanded. "Come now, don't be thhy. Introduthe yourthelvth." Xavier pointed at Irene. "Who are you?"

"Irene Chen."

"My couthin hath ethellent tathte. And you?"

"Haley Miller."

"You have hair like Rita Hayworth."

He pointed his pen at Devon. "You mutht be Devon McKnight, boy photographer. Tho, we are all prethent and accounted for. Letth get thtarted, thhall we, my little thpathe cadetth? Firtht quarter, Englithh—you're covering drama. Which jutht happenth to be my thpethialty. And you're thtarting with Thhakethpeare. Perfect."

Irene gave him a sheet of paper. "Here'th the

thyllabuth," she said, before blushing. "Sorry. It's sort of contagious. Like Shaun told you, we're reading *A Midsummer Night's Dream* first, because the drama club is doing a production of it this fall."

Xavier clapped his hands. "Yeth! *Dream* is ethellent comedy. Theater ITH life, you know. Thtudy theater, and you'll learn about the HUMAN THOUL. Ath the great Richard Burton once thaid, 'The theater bringth an actor down through the BLOOD and the MUD and the GUTTH, but if he survivth he'll EMERGE through the HIGHETHT REACHETH of the HUMAN THOUL into HEAVEN itthelf.' "

Haley and the other tutorees stared at him. Shaun said, "Xavier, man, what have you been smoking?"

"You're right, Thhaun," Xavier said. "Richard Burton never actually thaid that. I made up the quote, but itth THERTAINLY thomething he MIGHT have thaid. Now, do any of you have any theatrical ethperienthe?"

Haley glanced from Devon to Shaun to Irene, and they all stared back at her.

"Dude, you're jiving me, right?" Shaun exclaimed. "I mean, this is what passes for tutoring?"

"Right again, Thhaun," Xavier said. "I am JIVING you. Well, I wath GOING to thuggetht that you all try out for the play, thince thereth no better way to learn Thhakethpeare than to thpeak hith wordth ath he meant them to be thpoken—from the thtage. But *Dream* ith VERY challenging. If you've never acted before, you won't be catht. Tho, whatth the point of trying out?" He sighed and glanced at the syllabus again. "Too bad, becauthe I could have coached the HECK out of you. But you don't have it in you, do you? You don't have the COJONETH to TRY." He focused on Shaun as he passed them each a copy of the play. "You can read thith at home. We'll thtart with math today. A rather long math equathion."

Shaun's eyes shone as he flipped through the play. "Check this: there's a dude named Bottom in here."

"Yeth, yeth, Nick Bottom, HA-HA," Xavier said. "HILARIOUTH. But never mind that. Get OVER it. Never mind that Puck cathtth a thpell on him that turnth hith head into an arth'th."

"An ass for a head!" Shaun cried. "Awesome." A light seemed to flicker on behind his eyes.

"Uh-oh," Irene said. "I know that look."

"So do I," Devon said.

"What look?" Shaun said, fake-innocently.

"You had the same look when you decided to become the Evel Knievel of track and field," Devon said. "It's a look of crazed obsession. It's a look of unstoppability."

"This is not an obsession," Shaun insisted. "And it's not crazed. It makes perfect sense."

"WHAT are you all talking about?" Xavier said. "Fill me in, pleathe."

"I'm going to play Nick Bottom in the play this fall," Shaun said. "Just you watch me."

Xavier laughed. "Oh, Thhaun, Thhaun, Thhaun, that's a LAUDABLE goal, really. But you'll NEVER get the part. Not in a MILLION yearth."

"I'm serious," Shaun said. "Any dude named Bottom with a donkey's head is a dude I can relate to."

"But Thhaun, Bottom ith a major role," Xavier said. "You'll be up againtht kidth with MUCHO acting ethperienthe—maybe even PROFETHIONAL ethperienthe, knowing THITH nutty town. You don't have a chanthe."

"Watch me," Shaun said. He turned around, stuck out his chubby butt and slapped it. "Bottom—that's me. I was born to play this part, man."

"Oh my God," Irene said. "He's really going to do it."

"Not just me. You're all gonna be in the play with me," Shaun said. "Right, Rini?"

"I don't know, Shaun," Irene said. "Drama club is just the kind of thing I've tried to avoid all these years."

"It would look pretty good on our college transcripts," Haley added.

"That'th thertainly true," Xavier said. "That ith, if you don't get laughed off the thtage."

Precisely what Irene seemed to be afraid of. Drama club? Haley had never even thought of acting before. Did she have any talent? Did any of them? This looked like a recipe for either schoolwide fame or utter humiliation. Shaun was used to public embarrassment—thrived on it, even—but Haley preferred to keep her missteps as private as humanly possible, and she had a feeling Irene and Devon shared those sentiments.

"Come on, you guys, who's with me?" Shaun flipped through the play. "Look, there's a queen of the fairies—perfect for you, McKnight—and wood-land creatures and all kinds of great parts for you girls. We'll rock the school! Take over from the in-side. Those drama geeks won't know what hit them."

Xavier cleared his throat. "Ethcuthe ME, but I find the term *drama geek* offenthive."

Shaun rolled his eyes. "What do you say, kids? Going to join me on the boards? Will we see our names in lights?"

"I guess I'm in," Irene said. "I mean, why not, right?"

"If you guys are in, I'll try out too," Devon said. "Goodness knows I need something to put on my college application."

"What about you, Miller?" Shaun trained his crazed eyes on Haley. "I'll be an ass. But will you be a chicken?"

● ● ●

It looks as if Irene and Devon may be catching Shaun's strain of the theater bug. But is Haley ready for the spotlight? Come to think of it, is Shaun? Ready or not, he's found his new obsession. But that doesn't mean Haley has to follow in his chunky footsteps.

To invite more dramatic ups and downs into Haley's life, flip to page 64 (TOTAL DRAMA). If you think Haley should know what her natural talents are by now and focus on her sporty side, send her to soccer practice on page 57 (FOR KICKS).

Life is full of drama, not only on the stage. But thethpianth, as Xavier calls them, usually know how to live large. Acting in the play could bring a new dimension into Haley's life—or it could so overload her schedule that she wears herself out. How much can Haley handle? How far she gets pushed out of her comfort zone is up to you.

One strong look can be more convincing than a thousand words.

"Can you believe Sebastian and Mia are really coming back to school tomorrow?" Annie Armstrong asked, leading Haley to a front-row seat in the classroom where the debate team was practicing. The answer was no, Haley could not believe she would soon be running into the stunning Spanish couple in the halls. And she would rather not have to keep thinking about it either. "I'm so glad you decided to try out," Annie added. "Alex is going to love you! You're a shoo-in for first squad."

"Who's Alex?" Haley said, but Annie ignored her, striding to one of the two speaker's podiums at the front of the room. Standing beside her was a bookishly cute guy with short brown wavy hair. He was tall, with broad shoulders, and he wore crisp khakis and a tucked-in blue-pin-striped button-down shirt. With a bow tie. *Uh-oh,* Haley thought, intrigued in spite of herself. She had never before noticed this ultraconservative student at Hillsdale High, which was odd because she was sure she'd remember someone with such odd dressing habits, not to mention those dreamy hazel eyes. The boy's hair was parted on one side, and he had a stern, *Meet the Press* expression on his olive-skinned face. *He must be a senior,* Haley thought, accounting for his exoticism.

"If you could all take a seat," the boy said, banging a gavel on the podium. "Annie and I will get started. Welcome to debate team tryouts. I'm Alex Martin, captain of the team, and this is my cocaptain, our first-ever junior in the office, Annie Armstrong."

Annie, wearing a pale pink skirt and vest over a crisp white blouse, with a yellow headband in her ironed-straight hair, smiled and bowed slightly, even though no one had applauded.

"Annie will be handing out debate topics, and today you'll each have an opportunity to debate one of us and show us your skills," Alex said. Annie started handing out pieces of paper folded in half. Haley opened hers. *Topic: environmental policy. Resolved: the economic needs of the business community should be sacrificed for the sake of the environment. Your stance: pro.*

Hmm, Haley thought. This topic was perfect for her—almost too perfect. Her mother was a lawyer specializing in environmental issues, so Haley was well versed in the arguments on both sides. Annie, whose mother was a partner in the law firm where Mrs. Miller worked, must have known this and chosen Haley's topic to give her the best chance of making the team.

"First up, Whitney Klein will debate Annie," Alex announced. "Whitney?"

Haley was shocked to hear ditzy Whitney's name called. She was the last person on earth Haley would have expected to find trying out for the debate team. But then, with all the pressure to beef up credentials this semester, juniors were scrambling to participate in any and every activity that would help get them into college.

Annie took her place behind the podium on the left, while Whitney, stumbling to the front of the classroom in her bronze spike-heeled sandals, stood to the right. She smiled flirtatiously at Alex as he sat down at a desk with his gavel. Haley felt a bit jealous, and she was glad when Alex paid Whitney no mind. "Okay, begin," he commanded matter-of-factly.

"Resolved," Annie read from a pile of papers on

her desk. "Teenaged girls above the age of sixteen should be allowed to get breast implants without parental permission. My position is pro: a sixteen-year-old girl is old enough to know what she wants and should be allowed control over her own body. If she wants bigger breasts and can afford to pay for the surgery, she should be allowed to do whatever she likes within the limits of the law, even if her parents disapprove. Whitney?"

Whitney nodded and said, "I agree."

Alex snickered.

"No, Whitney, you're supposed to take the con position," Annie said. "See? What does it say on the paper I gave you?"

Whitney blinked at the piece of paper in her hand. "It says con. Oh. But that's not how I feel. I think girls should be able to get implants if they want. Why should their parents be able to boss them around?"

"No, Whitney, you're not getting the point," Annie said. "This isn't about how you really feel. You have to debate the side that's given to you, no matter what your personal opinions. It's an exercise in the ability to construct a logical argument. I personally don't think girls should be allowed to get implants at all, but my assignment is to argue pro."

"What?" Whitney said. "That doesn't make any sense. Why don't we just switch sides?"

Alex rolled his eyes and banged his gavel.

"Thank you, Whitney Klein. The exit is at the back of the room. Next up, Haley Miller will have the pleasure of debating yours truly."

Whitney tottered away from the podium. "So I didn't make the team?"

Annie shook her head. "Sorry, Whitney."

Whitney sighed. "That's okay. I think I still have time to make the spelling team tryouts."

"Good luck with that," Alex said as Whitney left. He took his place behind the left podium as Haley got up out of her seat. Annie moved to the desk with the gavel.

"Watch out for that guy," a dark-skinned kid named Dale from Haley's grade whispered as she walked to the front of the room. "He's been all-state three years running. They call him the Trail of Tears because he's made so many of his opponents cry."

"Resolved," Alex read, once Haley had taken her post. "The economic needs of the business community should be sacrificed for the sake of the environment. Haley takes pro."

"Thank you, Alex," Haley said in a strong voice. "The environment should always take first priority over the needs of big business. In fact, it's in the corporate interest to operate in an ethical and sustainable manner. Business needs natural resources to fuel growth and supply product to its consumers. And without healthy workers and healthy customers, economies would collapse. Therefore, while in the short term it may be less profitable to adopt environmentally sound practices, in the long run, everybody wins."

Annie rapped once with her gavel. "Thank you, Haley, time's up. Now Alex will present the con argument."

"Thank you, Annie." Alex cleared his throat. "Haley, your arguments have been reiterated by ignorant tree huggers for generations now. That doesn't make these sophistries any less ridiculous."

Haley felt the hair stand up on her forearms. How dare he insult her intelligence! She opened her mouth to protest, but Annie shook her head subtly. It wasn't Haley's turn. She had to sit through Alex's rant and wait until it was time for her rebuttal.

"If big business is forced to upgrade to cleaner technology overnight, you won't have to wait for supply chains to run out or natural resources to be depleted," Alex argued. "Economies will collapse instantaneously. Market equity will evaporate. Corporations will enter bankruptcy. We will lose our ability to harvest, process and transport food at a rate that can sustain our current worldwide population density. In the midst of such economic chaos and disorder, disease would spread and we would enter another era of plague. So in summation, the economy is far more important than our grasslands or forests. For what do forests and grasslands give us, anyway, if we can't strip them of trees to make the paper we need in a bustling economy, or graze cattle on them to nourish our citizens with protein? This country was built on allowing big business unfettered use of this great land. If that means a few seals have to die because we need to drill for oil in Alaska, so be it."

Ding! Annie rang the bell. "Haley—rebuttal?"

Haley had to tell herself to close her mouth, since her jaw had dropped open in astonishment at the brazen selfishness of Alex's argument. Alex had to be the most irritating person Haley had ever met. But— and she would never have admitted this to anyone out loud—she couldn't help but find him devastatingly handsome as he stood there glaring at her with such gusto and zeal. "Driving gas-guzzling SUVs is not a basic human right," Haley replied. "It's a luxury—a luxury that we must learn to do without before the entire planet is destroyed by our brazen, ignorant, piggish arrogance. What will happen when global warming causes the oceans to flood the coasts? How will your big businesses make money when their New York headquarters are swamped under a tidal wave? Business cannot afford to be shortsighted. We must think of the future, and that means preserving and caring for the planet. Not stripping it of everything we can take."

Ding! "Alex?"

"Global warming is a myth. I challenge you to provide me with one ounce of indisputable proof that our use of carbon fuels has caused any permanent damage to the atmosphere."

Haley couldn't believe this guy. "It's people like you who are destroying the earth!" she shouted before she could stop herself. "You're blind to the truth because all you can see is your own selfish greed!"

"I've heard enough," Alex said. "Haley just got personal. She obviously doesn't have a grasp of the rules of debate. No emotion allowed. She's too hotheaded to make a good debater. Sorry, Ms. Miller, but you're not qualified to join the team."

"What?" Haley was stunned. He was making a judgment now, just like that, without even hearing the rest of the tryouts? How dare he call her unqualified, just because he disagreed with her! "You're the one who's taking things personally!"

Annie shushed Haley and banged her gavel on the desk. "Overruled!" she shouted. "As cocaptain, I am revoking your vote, Alex. Haley Miller still has a lot to learn, but she's got eloquence and passion. She's in."

● ● ●

Thanks to Annie, Haley can now debate to her heart's content. But does she really want to? Where did arguing ever get anyone, anyway?

And what's with this Alex guy? Does he really believe that stuff he was spouting about baby seals? Or is

he just a very talented and objective debater? Could anyone be so hard-hearted? And what is it about him, aside from those hazel eyes, that Haley finds so attractive? Why does he get her head in such a twist?

Speaking of being tongue-tied, Spanish superbod Sebastian Bodega is back in town. The question is, are he and Mia still an item? If you think Haley wants to give Alex a chance to show a less aggressive side, and to see what Sebastian is up to, go to page 83 (SPANISH FLY). If you think Haley should probably stay away from Alex and the whole debate team and find a less stressful extracurricular activity, go to page 95 (OPEN MIKE). Finally, if you think Haley needs more time to make up her mind, turn to page 90 (THE BAG LADY).

Is Haley really wanted on the debate team? Or will Alex just keep baiting her? And will this line of questioning bring her pain, or gain? Read on to find out.

True or false: If you think too hard, you could pull a muscle in your brain.

Finally, Haley thought with relief when she at last spotted the door marked MW 341: MATH OLYMPICS. She'd just spent ten minutes wandering through the notorious maze of corridors that was the math wing. It wasn't her best time, but at least it was an improvement on the appalling half hour it had once taken her to get to geometry class.

Haley paused before opening the door. Sure, Reese was inside waiting for her, but was she really cut out to compete in the Math Olympics? She knew her way around a quadratic equation, but solving for x as the clock ticked down to zero, in front of ten or twenty intimidating adults and peers? This wasn't exactly an activity Haley had ever imagined herself excelling at. But, her hottie neighbor had suggested that they compete together, and her transcript did need the help, so she was beginning to think it was worth at least a try.

Haley opened the door and found herself standing in a typical classroom, with dry-erase, chalk- and bulletin boards on three walls; one wall was lined with windows that looked out onto the math wing's enclosed rotunda. The building had been constructed to architecturally mimic the double-helix structure of DNA.

Reese was at the head of the room consulting with a lanky, long-faced man in baggy pants, a lumpy sweater vest and owlish glasses. The man was stabbing at a piece of paper with a pencil. "No, no, no, you've got the parabolic curve in the negative quadrant," he thundered, clearly annoyed at this rare mistake on Reese's part. "Your data is all askew, Highland." Haley accurately guessed that this was the famed AP calculus teacher, Cosmo Milosevic, who was known for tearing down his pupils completely before building them back up, sometimes into award-winning mathematicians. He'd sent a student to a national chess competition the previous fall. Mr. Milosevic was checking Reese's work aloud—public scrutiny was just one of his effective sharpening tools—and Reese was so engrossed in the critique, he didn't even notice Haley standing by the door.

"Ahem," she said, clearing her throat to no avail. Haley couldn't help feeling a little disappointed. She'd hoped that this after-school activity would bring her closer to Reese, but here in the math wing, he wasn't even acknowledging her presence. *What did I expect?* she thought. *Balloons, confetti and roses?*

Haley felt herself inching backward toward the exit. Reese hadn't seen her yet. It wasn't too late to back out . . . but then something, or rather someone, caught her eye. There was a wave of acknowledgment from the back of the room. The palm in the air belonged to a bookish guy with short brown hair parted on the side and intelligent hazel eyes. He wore an ultraconservative blue button-down shirt tucked into stone-colored khakis, with a dark brown belt and loafers. And yet the effect of this look wasn't at all dorky. His tie was loosened and hung limp about his neck, and the top two buttons of his collar were undone. Haley didn't recognize him immediately, so figured he must be a senior. And a cute one, she thought, immediately drawn to him. Grateful he seemed to be summoning her over, Haley walked across the classroom and made a beeline for him.

"Hi, I'm Haley," she whispered.

"Huh? Oh, I'm Alex, Alex Martin," the boy replied, still staring straight ahead. Haley recognized the name from a flyer she had seen earlier that day advertising tryouts for the debate team, of which Alex was cocaptain with Annie Armstrong.

"Do we know each other?" Haley asked.

"You were blocking the chalkboard," Alex said harshly, without so much as a nod in her direction. "Do you mind? I'm in the middle of an important proof."

Haley felt like an idiot. *So this one couldn't care less either,* she thought, blushing profusely. Haley took out her graphing paper and began working on some of the minor problems that were written on the board. After a few minutes, she got restless and scanned the room. *Of course my only female compatriot in this sea of socially awkward eggheads is Hannah Moss,* she thought. Hannah and some of the students sitting nearby were all wearing matching nylon jackets with NUMBERS ONLY printed on the left-front pockets—there to hold pens, pencils and their all-important calculators. *Ugh, what am I doing here?* Haley thought, exasperated, as Reese continued his deep conversation with Mr. Milosevic and Alex remained intent on his scribbling. *Better yet, what's Reese doing here? He doesn't exactly fit the Math Olympian profile. I mean, do any of these brainiacs even realize who he is?* She looked around, and not a single math club geek seemed to care that the junior class's most smoking member was in their midst. Maybe that was part of why he liked coming here, she realized. No one worshiped him here—he was just another guy with a tabulation pad.

And here, Haley Miller wasn't a prospective girlfriend. She was a teammate who needed to be able to hold her own in competition.

Okay, focus, Miller. You're here to study and improve your mind, not get a date for Saturday night. But in spite of this mature frame of mind, a girlishly reassuring and not unmathematical thought suddenly popped into her brain. *The guy-to-girl ratio at math club is fifteen to one! That has to work in my favor!*

Consoled just a little, Haley couldn't help but smile and think that this just might turn out to be fun—even though Reese remained oblivious as he came and took the desk next to her, and Alex didn't say another word to her throughout the rest of the math club meeting.

● ● ●

Haley understands the notion of getting lost in your work, but this is ridiculous. Doesn't Reese realize there's competition in his midst? Haley seems to be taking a shine to this senior smartie. Is her affection for him greater than, less than or equal to her affection for Reese? When it comes time to submit results, which math wizard will win Haley's heart? Or will they both continue to ignore her in favor of their work?

If you think Haley should forgive Reese this momentary lapse in manners, go to page 95 (OPEN MIKE). If

you want to give Haley more time to think things over—
and perhaps change partners—go to page 90 (THE BAG
LADY).

Reese had better watch out. He's not the only head
for numbers in this town.

A captain must be able to rally the troops, on and off the field.

On her way to soccer practice, Haley spotted Sasha Lewis in the parking lot, tossing her backpack into the grooviest little red Mustang Haley had ever seen.

"Where'd you get the wheels?" Haley asked.

Sasha shut the car door and leaned against the hood, grinning in her navy shorts and gold and blue Hillsdale Lady Hawks T-shirt. "Isn't he gorgeous?" she said. " I call him Stallion. He's a vintage sixty-nine Mustang. A birthday present from Pascale."

Sasha, whose mother, Pascale Lewis, was French

and *très* chic, had recently turned seventeen, which in New Jersey was the legal driving age. Haley could hardly wait until her next birthday, in February. But having friends who could drive was almost as good as being able to drive yourself.

"Stallion, eh?" Haley said as she checked out the black leather bucket seats. "Sweet."

"Boys are always naming their cars after girls," Sasha said. "But this car feels like a boy to me. And I can drive him wild."

"Totally," Haley said, pulling a flyer off Sasha's dash. "What's this?" She glanced quickly at the printed message. "Open tryouts for *A Midsummer Night's Dream*. Are you thinking of entering the theater, too?"

"No way. Are you kidding? I've got enough on my plate. But you, on the other hand—I could see Haley Miller busting out some acting chops. You act all shy, but secretly you know you want the spotlight." Haley blushed.

On the field, Coach Tygert blew his whistle. "Lewis! Miller! Let's move it!"

Sasha and Haley jogged onto the field in their cleats for the first varsity girls' soccer practice of the year. "Looks like Tygert's still married," Sasha said as a flash of sun glinted off the gold ring on the coach's left hand. "Too bad."

"Yeah, she's a lucky woman," Haley said, swooning.

"Okay, girls, welcome to a new season of varsity soccer," the coach said. "We've got a great group this year and in spite of last year's end-of-season meltdown, I think this team can take it all the way."

The girls clapped and cheered. "Woo-hoo!" "All right!" "Go Hawks!"

"But first things first," Coach Tygert said. "As you all know, Tanya and Padma graduated last year, so we need a new team captain. Tessa and Jen are our only returning seniors—" He nodded at two girls who had spent more time on the bench last year than on the field. Jen nodded smugly, as if the captaincy were hers by default. *Not so fast, Jen,* Haley thought. Tessa ducked her head as if she hoped no one would notice her—clearly not eager to lead the team to victory.

"The job is open to anyone you think is qualified," Coach Tygert finished. "So . . . nominations?"

A perky sophomore named Christina raised her hand. "I nominate Sasha. Look, Sash, we were all a little pissed off at you last year when you blew off our final game. But you've proven yourself over the summer. I've never seen anyone so dedicated to this team. I think you've earned our trust back. And come on, we need you. Your skills are wicked good."

"Second," another sophomore shouted triumphantly.

"I nominate myself," Jen said forcefully, when no one else called her name.

"Okay, that's allowed," said Coach Tygert. "I like to see confidence in a leader."

"Haley Miller," a junior named Dee chimed in. "She and Sasha are our best players. No offense, Jen," she added, looking in the annoyed senior's direction.

"Any other nominations?" Coach Tygert asked. The girls were quiet. "No? All right, let's vote. The three nominees are Sasha, Haley and Jen. Nominees, turn around, please, so the voters won't be intimidated by your scorching glares."

The girls laughed as Haley, Sasha and Jen turned around on the bleachers, their backs to the rest of the team. "All right," Haley heard the coach saying. "Who votes for Jen? Hands? Okay. Sasha?"

Haley thought she heard more movement this time, more of a rustle, but it was hard to tell.

"Now, last but not least, hands for Haley."

Haley glanced at Sasha, who rolled her eyes and said, "Do you believe this foolishness?"

"I should be captain," Jen butted in. "Seniority should count for something."

"Okay, nominees, you can turn around now," Coach Tygert said. "Well, it looks like we have a tie. Haley and Sasha got nine votes each."

Haley was stunned. Her teammates looked up to her that much? She knew a lot of girls would vote for Sasha, but she hadn't expected to do just as well. She did the math in her head. That meant the whole team had voted for either Haley or Sasha—except for one. Haley was willing to bet that Jen's one vote had come from her fellow senior, Tessa.

"So I have a proposal," the coach said. "What do you think of Haley and Sasha as cocaptains? Since they're both busy juniors, they could share the responsibility."

"Yeah!" the girls shouted.

Sasha shrugged. "Cool with me."

"Me too," Haley said.

"Excellent," Coach Tygert said. "Girls, meet your new leaders, Sasha and Haley!" He held up an arm of each girl in a victory salute. Haley felt her face turn red. She was embarrassed but thrilled at the same time. She and Sasha got along great, and being cocaptains of the varsity soccer team would look awesome on their college applications.

"I'll have *Captain* embroidered on your team jackets," the coach said. "You should get them next week. Okay, three laps around the field and then we'll scrimmage. Go!"

Christina clapped Sasha and Haley on the back. "Congrats! You guys will be awesome."

"Thanks," Haley said. She fell into step beside Sasha as they jogged around the field.

"You busy after practice tomorrow?" Sasha asked.

"What, you mean besides having a jillion hours of homework and a thousand SAT vocabulary words to memorize?" Haley said. "Not really. Why?"

"I'm playing open mike at Drip," Sasha said. "Busting out some new material I worked on over the summer. I could sure use a little support, a friendly face or two. Those open mike crowds can be brutal. What do you say?"

● ● ●

Good for Haley—she's racking up the accomplishments and her high school transcript is looking more impressive by the minute. Who knows—as cocaptain of the soccer team, could she be lining herself up for a future athletic scholarship? Unfortunately, even student-athletes can't neglect the student part of the equation, though. Sasha is burning the candle at both ends, as usual. That doesn't mean Haley has to follow in those sometimes less-than-graceful footsteps. On the other hand, good friends—and cocaptains—support each other. So what should Haley do?

If you think Haley is curious to hear Sasha's new songs (maybe some of the lyrics are about people she knows!), take her to Drip for OPEN MIKE on page 95. If you think Haley has a budding actress inside her dying to get out, and she can always see Sasha sing another time, send her to page 102 to try out for *A Midsummer Night's Dream* (ON A ROLE). If you think Haley shouldn't make any more decisions before she straightens out her wardrobe for fall, send her to page 90 (THE BAG LADY).

Junior year is crammed with activity, but no one can do it all. Choose carefully, or Haley could find herself falling down a rabbit hole.

Good acting takes a lot of effort, but sometimes it's harder just being yourself.

"We'll show Xavier," Shaun shouted, his voice muffled by the huge papier-mâché donkey's head that was covering him from the shoulders up. "We're all gonna get huge parts, and take over the drama program from the inside out. No one's gonna believe how crazy delicious we are onstage. The theater crowd is gonna love us." Devon had to keep pointing Shaun in the right direction as they walked toward the auditorium. In full costume, Shaun couldn't exactly see straight.

"Well, no one can say we lack commitment," Irene said, lifting up the skirts of her long ivory antique satin gown to step over a puddle. Irene's gold crown completed an ensemble that was most definitely fit for a fairy queen. She looked regal enough for the part.

Devon, who worked at a vintage clothing store called Jack's, had helped them all scrounge up appropriate Shakespearean costumes for their *A Midsummer Night's Dream* auditions. Haley was surprised at how committed Devon himself had become to landing a role in the production. An artist and photographer, he'd always been the stern, quiet type, preferring to observe the Hillsdale High circus through a lens rather than draw attention to himself and actively participate. Now here he stood, in gym bloomers tricked up to look like Elizabethan breeches, yellow tights and a purple ruffled shirt. *Maybe he's finally coming around,* Haley thought, admiring her beau in his period getup. He'd even dug up the perfect dress for Haley to wear, a navy velvet gown with gold trim and mutton sleeves.

Shaun topped them all, of course, with the donkey's head he'd made in Mr. Von's art class—unfortunately built without working eyeholes—worn over a green makeshift leotard covered in leaves, crafted out of three discarded Peter Pan costumes. The leotard was a tad small for Shaun, but somehow that protruding Willkommen belly crammed into spandex seemed a good touch for the character of Nick Bottom.

"I understand the ways of the ass," Shaun chanted under his mask. "I feel the ass growing within. I am becoming the ass!"

"No surprises there," Devon joked.

"Cut the Method crap, Shaun," Irene said. "I can't take any more chanting."

Xavier, Shaun's cousin and their new after-school tutor, had told them all about Stanislavsky's famous acting method, used by Marlon Brando, James Dean and other legends of stage and screen. "The actor mutht find the character heth playing inthide himthelf," Xavier had said. "Digging deep, deep, deep inthide and living the life of that character in every detail until he BECOMETH the part. He doethn't PLAY the character; he ITH the character. They are ONE. Intheparable."

"It's all about technique, Rini," Shaun said. "I was born to play Bottom, and I'll do whatever it takes. And you shall be my queen." He took Irene's hand and kissed it with his papier-mâché donkey lips.

"Well, I hope this isn't all for nothing," Irene said. It was a bold move for someone who'd never been in a play before to go out for the part of Titania, queen of the fairies and Bottom's love interest. Titania was one of the female leads, a star of the show, and potentially the best part for a girl in the play.

The play's characters came from two different worlds, the human world and the fairy world. Haley planned to audition for a major human role, Helena or Hermia, mostly because Devon had declared his intention to play Lysander or Demetrius. These two couples switched partners during the play, so if Haley and Devon both got parts, the odds were pretty high that they would be canoodling onstage. Method acting or no Method acting, playing love scenes opposite Devon was definitely something Haley could manage. If all worked out, of course.

"It's just a silly school play," Devon said to Irene as they neared the auditorium. "How competitive could it be?" Then he opened the door, and the four friends gasped at what they saw. The auditorium was full of aspiring actors and actresses, studying their scripts and running lines in preparation for their staged reads in front of the drama coach. Each major character's name was written on a separate poster at the front of the auditorium, and behind the names, lines of potential cast members snaked through the aisles. There were hordes of people there to try out for Helena and Lysander and Oberon and Puck, of course, but the line for Titania stretched all the way to the door. On the other hand, only a handful of kids had signed up to attempt the role of Bottom.

"Good grief," Irene said, her face even paler than usual. "Look at all those wannabe fairy queens."

Haley, too, had forgotten about the Hillsdale

effect. Basically, in order to do anything at all ambitious at such a large public school, you first had to compete with a mob of supertalented, super-qualified, cutthroat kids. There was even heavy competition for slacking off, ever since Annie Armstrong and Dave Metzger had made lazy ennui fashionable among the type-A set.

"But you're the only one dressed for the part," Shaun said reassuringly to Irene. "Old Lyons can't resist the Mistress with the Method."

"Maybe Shaun has a point," Haley said. "You're committed, and your costume proves it."

Still, the threatened look in Irene's eyes did not escape any of them. Irene looked down at her satin gown and stifled a shriek. "Are you crazy? I look like an idiot!"

"Come on, Titania," Shaun said, trying to coax her into the role. "Normally, I wouldn't think that's such a good look, but from the ass's eye view it's wicked awesome."

"The ass's eye view!" Irene said. "Who cares about that?"

"That's exactly what Titania would say! If she talked all normally and not Shakespearean-like," Shaun offered.

"Everybody's nervous, Irene," Devon said. "Don't worry. You'll be great."

But Haley was afraid Irene had a first-class case of stage fright. Irene's hands were shaking, her eyes were huge, and they kept darting around the room. She seemed on the verge of a major freak-out.

"I—I can't do it," Irene stammered. "I'll make an ass out of myself."

"That's the whole point," Shaun said. "At least in my case."

"Shaun, shut up," Haley said.

Irene heaved her green army-surplus backpack over her shoulder and said, "I'll see you guys later." Then she hurried out of the room.

Shaun, Devon and Haley frowned at each other.

"Wow," said Devon. "She's really tripping."

"I'll make sure she's okay," Haley said, and chased Irene to the girls' bathroom. Irene had already run into a stall and pulled the satin gown over her head. Now she was diving back into her comfy ripped white tee.

"Are you all right, Irene?" Haley asked.

"I am now," Irene said with a sigh. "I'm sorry, but it's just too much in there. Did you see who was in line for Titania? Coco De Clerq, about a dozen seniors and that new Spanish chick, Mia Delgado, who I've heard is in, like, three television commercials this month."

"Mia?" Haley hadn't had time to check out the room. But if Irene was right and Mia Delgado had been there, that meant the rumors were true— Sebastian Bodega was back from Spain, and he had his luscious girlfriend-slash-model, Mia, in tow. That much Spanish spice could not be good for the delicate constitution of Hillsdale High.

"Yeah," Irene said. "The one with the legs up to her armpits. How am I supposed to compete with that?"

My sentiments exactly, Haley thought, hoping that Devon wasn't out there ogling the Latin stunner. "Maybe you're doing the right thing," Haley said. "I'm not so sure any of us is cut out for the theatrical life."

● ● ●

Well, that scene was certainly dramatic. Maybe Irene isn't giving herself enough credit. Since when does she get so emotional in public? And what will Irene do if Shaun lands the role of Bottom, and Coco De Clerq or Mia Delgado ends up playing his love interest?

Did Irene really spot Mia trying out for Titania? The girl is still learning English as a second language, and already she's tackling Shakespeare? Are Mia and Sebastian still an item? And how many hearts will Mia break before the school year is through?

Haley has got a lot to think about here. The production could be a great experience and might impress college recruiters down the line. But between classes, tutoring and everything else she has on her plate, where will Haley find the time to memorize her lines? How many words can she stuff into her brain before it explodes? On the other hand, Haley's playing opposite the adorable Devon could take their relationship to the next level. That is, if Haley can beat out all those more experienced actresses who are up for the part.

If you think Haley needs to clear her head with a good shopping spree before she makes a final decision, go to page 90 (THE BAG LADY). If you think there's no doubt she's cut out for the theater and a little drama is just what she needs, send her to page 102 (ON A ROLE). Lastly, if you think Haley's biggest worry should be the status of Sebastian and leggy Mia, go to page 83 (SPANISH FLY).

Fate may play a big role in Shakespearean drama, but in this drama you're the playwright. You get to write your own entrance.

Politicians are always
surrounded by throngs of
obsequious supporters.
It doesn't necessarily mean
they're well liked.

A finely tuned engine roared as Haley shielded her
eyes from the sun to peer into the parking lot of
the Bergen County Country Club. Not surprisingly,
Spencer Eton was at the wheel. He raced up the drive
in his brand-spanking-new, bright blue precision
Italian sports car—a gift for his recently turning
seventeen, legal driving age in New Jersey, and for
his efforts in service of his mother's campaign.

"The early bird has landed," Coco De Clerq said
with a sigh. "He certainly doesn't inherit his sense of

punctuality from his mother." Mrs. Eton, in fact, had been inside for a full forty-five minutes, entertaining guests at her latest fund-raiser on her race to become the state's next governor.

Spencer hopped out of his ride and breezed up the steps of the country club and onto the veranda, where members and donors were having drinks and enjoying the Indian summer. The youngest member of the Eton clan was dressed with his usual preppy bravado, in a half-untucked pale blue button-down, tie flung over his shoulder, not-too-faded fine-wale corduroys and suede desert boots. He topped it all off with a crisp navy blazer and sandy blond hair freshly windblown from the open sunroof on the ride over.

Haley didn't trust Spencer as far as she could hit him with a polo mallet, but she had to admit, the sparkle in his emerald green eyes was pretty tough to resist. She could understand why even the ice queen Coco De Clerq had been thawed by that gaze.

"Girls, girls, girls," Spencer said, kissing Coco passionately on the cheek as he nearly swept her off her stilettos. He bent down to give Haley a peck hello too, but she dodged him.

"Hello, Spencer," she said, giving him a friendly wave instead. The last thing she wanted to do was provoke Coco's notorious jealous streak.

"How can Mother lose with such beautiful campaign workers flogging her noble cause?" Spencer asked, grabbing a plump grape from a passing fruit tray and popping it into his mouth.

"I am not here to flog your mother's cause," Haley said emphatically. She wanted to make sure Coco understood this too. Haley's Berkeley-minded parents would never vote for a rich conservative like Mrs. Eton, and they'd have an absolute fit if they thought Haley had become a cadet in her army of supporters. Haley was here only because Coco had invited her to the club for a much-needed study break post–SAT prep class, not mentioning of course that a campaign stop was part of the deal. It was such a beautiful Saturday, and after a morning spent cramming vocabulary words into her head, it was heaven to be outside in the fresh air.

"Of course she's going to help," Coco said, glaring pointedly at Haley. "You're late, darling," she added to Spencer, but fondly, not in her usual snippy way, much to Haley's surprise. "The election is only a month away, and Mother Eton has been losing steam in the polls." Coco was the picture of Waspy elegance in her yellow cashmere sweater and triple strand of creamy white pearls, her chestnut hair pinned up to make her look older and more responsible and trustworthy. In her arms was a basket of *Vote Eleanor* campaign buttons in a buttery yellow that nearly matched her sweater, and a stack of leaflets promoting Mrs. Eton's run for governor of New Jersey.

"Are you kidding? Mother's got it sewn up,"

Spencer replied in his usual cocky manner. He spotted Whitney, in a tweed pencil skirt of her own design and a tight ruffled blouse, standing by the bar. "Can I get you ladies a drink? Haley? Cocomo?"

"We'll have two Arnold Palmers," Coco ordered. Spencer brushed his hand through hers as he left for the bar, letting their fingers linger together a second longer than they needed to. Haley saw a warm gleam in Coco's usually chilly eyes. *Has Spencer finally been tamed?* Haley wondered, marveling at the change that had recently come over Hillsdale High's resident bad boy.

"He's whipped!" Haley announced to Coco, risking incurring her friend's wrath. She braced herself for the reaction. However, no wrath seemed to be coming.

"He's an old family friend, as you know," Coco said, mustering all her Grace Kelly restraint. "But yes, things have heated up a bit since my . . . sister finally left for Yale." Coco was the type of girl who wanted every boy to want her, but she'd always had a soft spot for Spencer. They seemed to be made for each other. Unfortunately, Alison De Clerq had maintained a long-standing and avid flirtation with her sister's beau. Even though the relationship had never been consummated, Coco felt that Ali—among others—stood in the way. Now, it seemed as if Coco might have been right.

The queen bee, finally restored to her throne,

smoothed her hair and stood at attention as Mrs. Eton fluttered over to greet the girls. "Thank goodness, another pair of hands," Spencer's mother said, plopping a load of buttons and flyers into Haley's arms. "Here you are, dear. Well, what are you waiting for? Get to work." Mrs. Eton then hurried over to the bar for a photo op with her handsome offspring. She had a beaming maternal grin plastered all over her nipped-and-tucked face.

"I'll take those off your hands," Whitney offered, setting down her Arnold Palmer. "It'll be easier for me to pass them around, since I know everybody here and you probably . . . don't."

Haley had to admit Whitney was right. "Thanks," she said, relieved to be rid of the offending Republican propaganda. Haley nevertheless felt the need to follow Whitney around on this hearts-and-minds-winning mission. Mostly, it was to get out of cozying up to the elderly gentlemen in attendance, a task Coco had just been tapped for. Haley cringed as she watched Coco lean down and speak into the good ear of a former club president, revealing all too much of her meager décolletage.

Haley and Whitney strode up to the first table, where a silver-haired couple was sitting beneath an umbrella. She wore frosty pink lipstick and a chunky beaded necklace that covered up her wattle, and a stiff tobacco-colored skirt suit. He had on his old college fraternity pin, an official-issue green country club blazer and a green and white repp tie. They both were sipping gin and tonics. "Vote for Mrs. Eton!" Whitney said brightly, placing a flyer and a button on their table.

"You're preaching to the choir," the woman said, picking up the yellow *Vote Eleanor* button and dropping it disdainfully back into the basket. "You can keep your button. I never wear political slogans on my person."

"I'll wear it," the old man said, snatching it back up and giving Whitney a wink. He heartily pinned it to his lapel, next to his Sigma Nu insignia. "If we support the woman, why not tell the world?"

"William, you look positively vulgar," the woman said.

This from a woman in plastic jewelry, Haley thought critically. She instantly felt guilty for her snobbish sentiments. *Must be contagious,* she realized, looking around at the setting.

"We have to keep moving, Dr. and Mrs. Burnham," Whitney said politely. "Give my best to your poodle Peaches, and have a lovely afternoon."

"As long as the gin is flowing, we will, dear," Mrs. Burnham said. "We will."

As Whitney and Haley made their way from table to table, Haley watched Spencer, who was now obediently following Coco's every move around the party, just as if he were the poodle.

"Coco can't wait to be the First Girlfriend,"

Whitney observed from a distance. "I bet she'd marry Spencer the day after the election if he'd have her, just so she could live in the governor's mansion and be part of New Jersey's ruling family."

"Come on," Haley said, scoffing. "You really think she'd consent to be a child bride?"

"All I know is, Coco loves the word *first,* especially when it's attached to her name," Whitney said. "Besides, it is Spencer we're talking about here." Spencer, who at that moment was leaning down to kiss an adorable towheaded baby. "Wouldn't you marry that?"

Haley glanced over at Spencer's mother, who seemed especially plastic as she leaned down to pose with a crippled World War II veteran. "And become the next Mrs. Eton? No way."

"Harsh," said Whitney, who couldn't help but giggle. "So I guess you heard Sebastian's back in town."

"Yeah, with Mia Delgado nipping at his heels," Haley said, annoyed that there would now be a full-fledged model roaming the halls at Hillsdale High.

"Can you believe it? I thought we got rid of her last spring, but apparently they spent the summer together in Miami, and now Mia's in our class, which seems to make the football team pretty happy. I was sort of thinking of asking her to be in the look book for my spring line. Do you think she would give a classmate a discount? Oh, what do I care. Daddy's back, and now he's footing all the bills. He doesn't seem to care if I'm in the red or the black, whatever that means." Whitney carelessly dumped a pile of buttons onto someone's table, having tired of her chore. Now that they were in gossip mode, Mrs. Eton's tax-reform plan was quickly forgotten. "Did you know Mia shot all sorts of ads and commercials in Miami this summer? They're a lot more liberal about nudity down there. I'm just saying."

Haley felt slightly sick to her stomach. There was a time when she'd thought she and Sebastian might have some potential as a couple. But Mia's arrival last year had put an end to those plans, and now here she was again, complicating everything, and posing a threat to every student at Hillsdale High who possessed two X chromosomes.

"I just can't stand the way guys look at her, you know?" Whitney said. "I mean, does she have to take, like, all of them? Couldn't she just flirt with the dweebs and leave the football team for me?"

Haley, in need of a palate cleanser, reached for a glass of water on a passing tray. "Can we change the subject?" She had a feeling Mia Delgado would be dominating conversation around Hillsdale for many months to come, and she wanted to put off the inevitable for as long as possible.

"Sure," Whitney said. "I'd rather gossip about Zoe Jones anyway. What happened to her, do you think? I could sculpt a pot out of all the plaster makeup she's got caked on these days. If you ask me, she was prettier before she started running around with Motormouth. Oh, you want to hear something really gross? Do you know what Sasha and Johnny did while camping in Virginia this summer?"

"Uh, since you prefaced it like that, no thanks," Haley replied. Whitney wasn't known as the most reliable source in town.

"How can Sasha like that greaseball?" Whitney continued, undeterred. "All I know is, they went down there with nothing but a tiny little pup tent. What do you think happens in a tiny little pup tent? Everything, obviously!"

"Obviously," Haley teased.

"And don't tell Cecily, but I heard from someone who heard from someone who said they saw Drew making out with a freshman at the cineplex over the summer. And I'm talking about a girl who's just a freshman now, not from Zoe's class. Why would he be such a dog to Cecily?"

"Are you sure that's true?" Haley said. "Drew and Cecily seem so . . . serious."

"That's why it's shocking," Whitney said.

"Of course," Haley added sarcastically.

"So what's the dirt on Reese?" Whitney asked. "He's been in such a grind ever since school started. Have you seen much of him?"

"I, uh," Haley began, not knowing exactly what

to say. "We sort of fell out of touch over the summer. I don't really know what he's up to lately. I think he's really concerned about the whole college thing." Haley nodded her head as if to convince herself this was the only reason for Reese's disappearance.

"Yawn," Whitney said. "I can't wait until all this college crap is over and we can get on with our real lives. I mean, the SATs? Come on! Could they be a bigger bore? How am I supposed to know a synonym for *prattle*? What does that word even mean anyway?"

Haley certainly knew.

● ● ●

Whitney has a lot of dish for Haley, but what of it is true? Unlike the SATs, taking an educated guess in this case probably won't get you to the bottom of the Hillsdale rumor mill. After all, Whit hasn't always been innocent herself. Is she just manufacturing all this gossip to draw attention away from her own past transgressions?

If you think Haley is itching to catch up with Sebastian Bodega, even if it means encountering the wily Mia, go to page 83 (SPANISH FLY). If you think Haley is bored with the political scene and ought to be seeking her own stage, have her go out for the school play on page 102 (ON A ROLE). Want to rekindle those dwindling flames with Reese Highland? Send Haley hopefully to find her man at the OPEN MIKE on page 95.

Finally, if you think Haley needs a chance to catch her breath and pull herself together, turn to page 90 (THE BAG LADY).

Haley's just a small-town girl living in a fishbowl world. Some of what she hears may be too much information. But then, the more you know, the easier it is to make decisions. In theory, anyway.

SPANISH FLY

How do you say "Step aside for the new girl" in Spanish?

"Haley! Annie! *Hola!*"

Haley and Annie spotted Sebastian Bodega in the rotunda on their way out of math class. It was the first time Haley had laid eyes on him since the end of sophomore year, and she had to admit he looked hotter than ever.

"Sebastian must have trained all summer," Annie whispered, gawking at the strong swimmer's physique. "Now that's a backstroke I'd like to see up close."

It was true; Sebastian's build was even leaner and more muscular than it had been the previous spring. Of course, those old familiar dark curls and warm brown eyes didn't hurt his overall impression either.

"Hi," Haley managed, trying hard not to seem too eager for the long-lost Spaniard's attention.

Just as Sebastian was about to respond, a kittenish voice purred, "Oh, it's you. Hah-ley, is it?" A rail-thin olive-skinned fifth appendage slithered out from behind Sebastian's back. Her name was Mia Delgado, and she was a budding international supermodel who also happened to be Sebastian's childhood girlfriend. Ever since the stick-thin mannequin had arrived in the United States, she hadn't strayed from "Sebbie's" side—a fact that annoyed Haley no end.

"Hi, Mia," Annie droned. "I see you're adjusting well to Hillsdale High. As official new-student ambassador for the junior class, I am obligated to say welcome, and offer you my services should you need any help navigating the campus."

"No thank you. I already have an excellent tour guide," Mia cooed, batting her lashes at Sebastian, her arm possessively sliding around his waist.

Haley had come to the rotunda to decompress between classes, but the sight of Mia now made relaxing in the sun a total impossibility.

"Ugh, if Mia's always talking about how great it is

to live in Spain, why did she move to New Jersey?" Annie muttered under her breath.

"Good question," Haley responded, forcing a smile to conceal her displeasure with Mia's sudden appearance.

It was an unseasonably warm day, and the rotunda was crowded with juniors and seniors enjoying their midmorning study breaks. Every male eye in the place was on Mia—that is, except for the pair belonging to senior Alex Martin, who had his nose deep in *The Brothers Karamazov*.

Thank goodness someone here has some taste, Haley noted, fondly admiring the cute conservative upperclassman. If it weren't for his far-right-leaning politics, Alex might have been Haley's soul mate. He was way smart, a member of the math team and also cocaptain of the debate squad, which he led with none other than Annie Armstrong. And then there were those clear hazel eyes and his firm build, toned by years of fencing and rowing crew. *Maybe it wouldn't be so bad to date a Republican,* Haley thought, imagining what Alex must look like under his tweed blazer and green patterned necktie. He was certainly a far cry from the other guys present, who were all tossing footballs, kicking soccer balls and generally doing everything they could think of to show off for the newest and most glamorous Hillsdale resident, Mia Delgado.

When Haley and Annie had entered the rotunda, they had barely caused a stir. Haley suddenly realized with a sinking heart that she'd now been at Hillsdale for a full year already. She was no longer the cute new girl, rousing everyone's interest. That title now belonged to Mia—and so, apparently, did Sebastian Bodega.

"How was your summer, Haley?" Sebastian's eyes twinkled with genuine interest now. Mia was sufficiently distracted by a pair of football jocks, who were showering her with compliments and asking her all about the modeling world. Sebastian was, for the moment, free.

"My summer was . . . not exactly scintillating," Haley replied, pursing her lips.

"*Scintillating:* brilliantly lively, stimulating or witty," Sebastian said, rattling off the definition.

"I see someone studied his SAT words over break." Haley was impressed. Sebastian had lost a bit of his accent, and his English was improving dramatically.

Haley looked away and thought she saw . . . *Was Alex Martin just ogling me?* she thought, blushing. Sebastian incorrectly interpreted this as flirtation on Haley's part.

"All I did was study this summer, apart from swimming laps and lifting," he said, flashing his dazzling white smile.

"Are you sure that's all you did?" Haley asked, annoyed, her eyes traveling in Mia's direction. "I heard Mia spent quite a lot of time modeling in Miami. Isn't that where you were training?"

"Well," Sebastian began, "she was adjusting to life in the U. S. How could I not help her with her . . . culture shock. Plus, there is a lot of work for models in Miami."

"How convenient," said Haley, stealing another look in Alex's direction, just in time to catch the senior staring back at her. Alex quickly looked down and resumed his reading. *He* was *ogling me!* Haley thought, unable to contain her excitement. She beamed, and Sebastian once again mistakenly thought Haley's smile was directed at him.

"Oh, Haley, how can I explain? Mia will always be . . . Mia. But you, you are different. You are new. And American. And exciting." He caressed her shoulder. Out of the corner of her eye, she could see that this was not going over well with Alex, who was now shoving his things into his backpack and hurrying out of the rotunda, well in advance of the bell.

"Not so fast, lover boy," Haley said, brushing Sebastian's hand aside. "You're taken. Remember?"

"Oh, Haley, sometimes I don't think so," Sebastian replied, nodding in Mia's direction. The model was feeling up the biceps of one of the meatheads while another jock lifted her heavy book bag off her shoulder.

"Sebbie, these nice boys are going to walk me to my next class. That's okay with you, isn't it?"

"Of course," Sebastian called out, trying not to sound peeved, but clenching his jaw just the same. "It is good you are making new friends!"

"Oh, and remember," Mia added, "I have, how you say . . . drama this afternoon."

"Ugh," Annie interjected. "I can't believe she scored the lead in *A Midsummer Night's Dream*. It's almost enough to ruin Shakespeare for me."

"Mia thinks this acting business will help her English," Sebastian said, wistfully staring at her retreat. "She also, it will not surprise you to know, may have ambitions at a Hollywood movie career."

"Sebastian, how was your summer, really?" Haley asked, sensing that Miami was not the palm-treed lovers' paradise she had previously thought it to be. "Mia must have been quite the sensation down there."

"She does . . . attract attention to herself," Sebastian conceded. "But what am I saying, I was focusing on swimming the whole time! It is not so glamorous, I know, but I hope it will pay off this year when the college recruiters come to see me compete."

"Keep telling yourself that, sweetie," Haley said, collecting her books and patting Sebastian's hand as the bell rang.

• • •

Mia Delgado has arrived in Hillsdale with all the subtlety of a steamroller—and she's about to flatten Haley's ego, along with that of every other girl at Hillsdale High who stands in the beautiful vixen's way. Understandably, Haley is threatened by the new diva on the block. But what exactly is going on between Mia and Sebastian? Rumors are flying—everything from barely speaking all summer to spending weeks frolicking seminude on the beach.

Perhaps Mia is an unstoppable force, and Haley should throw in the towel and try to forget the Iberian *modelo* even exists. Especially with that cute prepster Alex Martin eyeing Haley from a distance.

If you think the wisest course for our heroine is to hang with the brainy kids, turn to page 115 (IT'S DEBATABLE). If you think Haley should keep an eye on Mia's antics—and maybe even throw a wrench into her plans for total high school domination—have Haley nab a part in the school play on page 137 (CASTING CALL). Maybe you think what's really at stake here is Sebastian—does Mia have a firm hold on him or not? Is he still interested in Haley? Is Haley interested in him? Send her to the SWIM MEET on page 124 to find out.

Haley should have known she couldn't be the new girl forever. But the flavor of the month lasts only . . . a month. After that, it's time to find a more permanent identity—or get lost in the crowd.

THE BAG LADY

Handbags can be practical, pretty or political—but they always make a statement.

"**T**wo trips to the mall in one month," Haley's mother grumbled. "I should just rip off this *Protect the Pine Barrens* button from my lapel and replace it with an *I Support the Malls of America* pin."

"This was your idea, Mom," Haley said. Of course, Haley realized she might have had something to do with suggesting it.

Haley's old backpack was so worn it had a hole in the bottom—a tiny hole that Haley had "accidentally" poked at all summer until it got big enough for, oh, her house keys to slip through. Once the tear was of a suitable size, she gave it a test run by tossing her keys into the bag. They hit the floor in seconds. *Perfect,* she thought, putting the next phase of her plan into action.

One morning before school, Haley waited until her mother was in the kitchen before gathering up her things to leave. She then picked up her bag and slung it over her shoulder, just as the keys, on cue, dropped at Joan's feet.

"What was that?" Haley's mother said, frowning.

Haley bent down and picked up the keys. "Huh," she said. "How did that happen?" She turned over her backpack and made a big show of peering through the hole in the bottom as if staring down a bottomless abyss. "Hey, there's a hole in my backpack."

"I could install a magnet in there if you want, Haley," Mitchell said helpfully. "It will help keep your keys inside that holey backpack, where they belong. Plus, that way you can find them easily. They're always in the right place."

Haley gave a look intended to silence her gadget-minded little brother.

"Let me see." Joan took the backpack and examined it. "Maybe I can get this patched up somewhere."

Patched up? That was not in the plan. Backpacks were so over at Hillsdale. Everyone she knew, from the often fashion-challenged Annie Armstrong to the fashion rebel Irene Chen, had a different kind of bag for carrying around their tons of stuff—a statement bag, a huge shoulder bag that held everything one would need to live on for up to three days. Backpacks were for middle-schoolers.

"If you put a magnet in there you won't need to patch it," Mitchell persisted. "Unless of course the hole was big enough for the magnet to fall through. Then we would have a problem."

"No magnets," Haley said. "And no patches, please. Don't you know how many books I have to carry? It'll just tear again. I think I need a new bag." Joan frowned. "I'll pay for part of it myself," Haley offered. "With my summer babysitting money."

That clinched it. "I guess . . . ," Joan said, finally worn down. "I'll run you over to the mall after supper tonight."

Which was how they ended up roaming through stores that evening, in spite of Joan's complaints.

"I've had that backpack for three years, Mom. And I'll probably have this bag for three more. This is not an extravagant purchase," Haley rationalized. She was all for her mother's social justice and environmental awareness, but sometimes a bag was just a bag—something you needed to carry your stuff in. Or was it?

Joan went off to look for a new business suit—

work clothes used to win cases against corporate polluters being exempt from her anticonsumerist stance—while Haley browsed the accessories aisles. She saw several bags she liked, but she had only enough money for one. It was so hard to decide. There was a snappy white patent leather purse with a hip late-sixties vibe, perfect for an artsy, individual type like Irene Chen. Then there was a versatile black satchel, a timeless classic that would fit well in Coco De Clerq's wardrobe. The peach suede purse looked girlish and safe, like something Annie Armstrong would wear. And finally, Haley was tempted by a red-trimmed canvas tote, which was sporty and fun and reminded her of Sasha. Haley looked at the bags over and over. The school year was still young, and she wasn't quite sure what kind of bag she'd need. Which one would suit her junior-year persona?

● ● ●

What will it be? The bag Haley chooses now will determine her path for this, the most important of school years. Should Haley assert her artsy individuality? Have her buy the white patent leather bag and send her to try out for the play on page 142 (ACTING COACH). Maybe you think the canvas tote would be best. If so, go to the soccer game (FANCY FOOTWORK) on page 132. To stick with the academic, college-bound set, it's the peach suede purse and the debate team all the way

(IT'S DEBATABLE) on page 115. Or maybe you think Haley should opt for the elegant black satchel, in which case, turn to CASTING CALL on page 137.

You are what you eat? Maybe. You are what you wear? For sure—at least while you're wearing it. Or carrying it, as the case may be.

OPEN MIKE

Unlike at karaoke night, tone-deaf people are not welcome to take the stage at an open mike.

"I should not even be here," Reese Highland said as the gang trooped into Drip, the local coffeehouse, for Wednesday-afternoon Open Mike. "I've booked up my life with every possible activity, and even my homework has homework."

"Tell me about it," Haley groaned. "SAT prep is killing me. It's those endless practice tests, on top of soccer and everything."

"At least you don't have to round up a pack of clueless freshman klutzes and try to turn them into a passable cheerleading squad," Cecily Watson complained. "Have you seen this year's newbies? They're about as graceful as a herd of Clydesdales."

Eager to see Sasha debut her new songs at Open Mike, they all settled at tables in front of the stage and ordered coffees. Haley found herself in a crew with Cecily, now captain of the cheerleading squad; Cecily's boyfriend, football star Drew Napolitano; Sasha's rocker boy, Johnny Lane; and Reese. Still, the whole excursion had sounded like more fun than it was turning out to be. Everybody was so stressed about preparing for college that they couldn't seem to relax.

"Those girls are wearing me out," Cecily said. "I'm losing my pep. My pep, people! Though it would help if we had something to cheer about." She cast a sidelong glance at Drew.

"Hey, I'm doing what I can," Drew said. "I trained hard all summer. I can't help it if varsity football is weak this year. Turns out the seniors who graduated last year carried us more than we realized. I just hope the team is good enough to attract a few recruiters—or it's no college for me, baby. I sure ain't getting in on my grades."

"Why did I join the Math Olympics team?" Reese said. "What was I thinking? The first meet is next week and I'm going to make a total fool out of myself. I'm going to stand up in front of everybody and my mind will go blank. The admissions office at

Princeton, Harvard, Dartmouth and Yale will hear all about it and they'll laugh hysterically while tearing up my applications. I'm doomed."

"Oh, please," Haley said. Nothing tragic ever happened to golden boy Reese. "You'll be fine. I'm the one who's going to be laughed out of the Ivies."

Johnny Lane rubbed his eyes impatiently. "All this college talk is boring my brains out. You get in, you don't get in. Who cares? You can always go to state."

Haley gasped.

"How can we not care?" Cecily said. "Our entire future is on the line."

"The future will happen whether or not you go to Vassar," Johnny said. He clapped his hands and whistled. "Bring out Sasha! Sasha Lewis, let's go!"

The room was still filling with people. A group of sophomores, led by Zoe Jones, crammed into a corner booth, giggling and spitting water at each other. Zoe's hair stuck off the top of her head in two wild spikes, and a heavy dash of eyeliner made her catlike eyes even more feline, yet somehow she still managed to look beautiful. Maybe it was the red spandex bodysuit and tutu over combat boots. Haley had to admit the girl had a look of her own, especially for someone so young. She certainly didn't lack confidence—Zoe was already the lead singer in Rubber Dynamite.

"Look at them," Cecily said wistfully. "Laughing

like they haven't a care in the world. Remember sophomore homework? Sophomore year is like kindergarten."

"Leave them in peace," Drew said, eyeing Zoe, along with every other guy in the room. "Let them have their fun while they can."

"I remember fun," said Cecily. "Wait until next year. We'll be seniors, coasting along on a wave of senior cut days."

"We'll be tearing our hair out, waiting to hear on admissions," Reese said.

"Hey," Johnny said. "I believe I asked you all to cut it." He stretched his long, denim-clad legs into the aisle and closed his eyes. "I wish this show would start already. You can't even get a beer in this dump."

"Excuse me, but you are in my way." Haley looked up as Mia Delgado sauntered past their table, followed sheepishly by Sebastian Bodega. "Please, can you move your legs?"

Johnny opened his eyes and glared at Mia. "Go around. There's no room at this table anyway."

Mia gasped, giving a dramatic toss to her long brown hair. She was wearing even more makeup than usual; her eyes were lined and spackled with blue shadow. "American boys are so uncivilized." She walked around Johnny's table and sat down in a seat right in front of him, blocking his view of the stage.

"Show the lady some respect," Sebastian said mechanically to Johnny before taking a seat next to Mia.

"Whatever," Johnny said.

Mia turned around to glare at Johnny and fluffed her hair again. Then she said to Sebastian, "I'm sorry I was late to meet you, puppy, but I went to the auditions and had to wait such a long time for my turn!"

Haley didn't mean to eavesdrop, but she couldn't help perking up her ears at the word "auditions." That explained the huge hair and excessive makeup—Mia's attempt to project "fairy queen" from the stage. She, like everyone else at Hillsdale it seemed, was trying out for *A Midsummer Night's Dream*.

"How did you do, Miacita?" Sebastian asked.

"Wonderful!" Mia declared. "I was brilliant, of course, what do you think? You know that director, Mr. Lyons, perhaps he thinks I am too beautiful to be the lead."

"Too beautiful? That is impossible."

"You never know, Sebastian, you never know. What are these Americans thinking? Sometimes I just don't understand them."

Sebastian patted her slender knee. "You will get the lead, Miacita, I feel sure of it. When have you ever been denied something you wanted?"

Haley fumed as they laughed over this. It was true: Mia always seemed to get her shy, manipulative way. Thinking about Mia's commanding presence and refusal to ever hear the word *no,* Haley began to wonder what *she* herself wanted. Maybe she wanted to be in *A Midsummer Night's Dream,* too. Why not?

Actually, there were lots of reasons why not: soccer, school, SATs and everything else she had signed up for. Haley's time was stretched to the limit. But when she thought about it, all her activities seemed so prosaic. So dull. So typical. Maybe drama was just what she needed to spice up her transcript—and her life.

The auditions were going on all afternoon. If she hurried back to the auditorium now, she might make it in time to try out. Haley drained her coffee. This was it. Do or die. If she was going to make it to those auditions, she'd have to leave right this minute.

● ● ●

Is Haley nuts? How is she going to cram another activity—especially a time-consuming one like drama—into her packed schedule? If she gets a major part, that's going to mean a ton of memorization—on top of all the memorizing she's already doing for SAT prep. Plus endless hours of rehearsal time . . .

But then, her school record as it stands does lack zip. Zing. Zazz, if you will. If she's going to get into one of her top schools, she's going to need to stand out. And what college ever turned anyone down for doing too much?

If you think theater could add another dimension to Haley's transcript, send her to audition on page 137 (CASTING CALL). If you think Haley should streamline her life and stick to soccer, go to page 132 (FANCY FOOTWORK).

Sometimes life feels like one big open mike—trying new things in front of a hostile audience. It's scary, but if you pull it off, the rewards make all the frenzy worthwhile.

You shouldn't bother trying out unless you're willing to play a supporting role.

"Haley, you're trying out too?" Whitney asked as Haley walked into the mobbed auditorium.

"God, half the school is auditioning for this play," Coco said.

Frankly, Haley was surprised to see Whitney and Coco auditioning for *A Midsummer Night's Dream*. Neither one of them struck her as having the ability, or the desire, to impersonate anyone but her fabulous self. And Shakespeare was never high on their list of priorities—he ranked miles above math but well below makeup, clothes and hair.

"I thought it might be fun," Haley said noncommittally.

"Look at all those girls lined up for the lead," Coco said, examining her perfect pearly pink nails. "Why do they even bother? Don't they know it's a lost cause?" She looked up at Haley and added, dismissively, "You're not foolish enough to try out for the lead, are you?"

"I thought I'd go for Helena or Hermia," Haley said. "You know, we *H* names have to stick together. And that way, I'm less likely to miss a cue onstage."

Coco didn't laugh. "Good. You wouldn't have a chance." She opened her paperback copy of the play and started reading.

"Not that it makes any difference," Haley said, "but why not?"

Whitney pulled her aside. "Because you-know-who's father funded the production this year—again," she whispered, twitching an elbow in Coco's direction. "So they have to make him happy. And he won't be happy if she's not happy. And she won't be happy unless she gets the lead."

"Obviously," Haley said sarcastically. "Why even hold auditions at all? Maybe they should auction off the parts to the highest bidders."

Whitney let a little laugh slip out but cut it short when Coco glared at them.

"So you're going to be Titania?" Haley said.

"Ti-who?" Coco sniffed. "No. I told you, I'm going to be the star."

"Titania is the star," Haley said. "The queen of the fairies? It's the biggest female role."

"Of course," Coco said. "I knew that. And it makes total sense. I'm queen of the school. Why shouldn't I be queen of the fairies? Who knows more about ruling than me?"

"And what about Mia?" Haley said. She couldn't help herself. Mia got on her nerves, but Haley had a hunch Mia got on Coco's nerves even more. Coco, after all, had very delicate nerves.

"What about her?" Coco sneered.

"I heard she's trying out for Titania," Whitney blurted out.

"So did I," Haley said with a satisfied smile.

"So?" Coco said. "Does Titania have a Spanish accent? Shakespeare was a British playwright. This is an English play. I really don't think Mia is much competition for anyone."

"Actually, this production is taking place in Athens," Haley said. "Athens, Greece," she added for Whitney's benefit.

"You call this English?" Whitney scanned a page of the play with her finger. " 'Skim milk, and sometimes labour in the quern, and bootless make the breathless housewife churn; and sometime make the drink to bear no barm—' "

"Cut it out, Klein," Coco snapped. "You've heard of skim milk, haven't you? Not that you'd be caught dead drinking it . . ."

"It's so watery." Whitney sniffed. "Maybe I'll try out for Hermia. Isn't she the girl everyone's in love with?"

"Not everyone," Haley said. "Just Lysander and Demetrius."

"And you know who's trying for one of those two parts," Coco said. "Señor Sebastian. Among several other hotties."

"Awesome," Whitney said. "I could handle some, um, face time with Sebastian. Is there kissing? Please let there be kissing."

"If you get the part," Coco said, emphasis on the *if*.

"Sorry, Whit—I guess being Mr. Moneybags's daughter only gets you so many favors," Haley said. She noticed Devon McKnight in line to audition for Lysander or Demetrius too. Interesting. If she got Helena or Hermia, whom would she rather kiss— Devon or Sebastian? It was a question for the eyes.

"Does Titania get to kiss whoever Sebastian wants to be?" Coco asked Haley.

"I don't think so," Haley said.

"Whatever," Coco said. "As long as I don't have to play opposite that giant donkey head. Who is that anyway?"

Across the room, Shaun Willkommen caroused with Irene and Devon while wearing a papier-mâché donkey's head. *He must think it will help his chances of playing the weaver, Nick Bottom,* Haley thought—since Bottom spends half the play under a spell that turns his head into an ass's.

"Yuck, it's that mullet-head Shaun," Whitney said. "I'd recognize that potbelly anywhere. Ick, just look at him."

"Actually, I think Titania does have to kiss Donkeyhead," Haley said happily. "I mean, Bottom."

"Ew, the character's name is Bottom?" Coco said. "How disgustingly appropriate. Why would the lead want to kiss *that*?"

"It's right there in the play," Haley said, flipping through her copy until she found the part where Titania thinks she's in love with Bottom. Haley was beginning to hope Coco did get the lead—seeing her kiss Shaun's donkey mouth in front of the whole school would be delicious.

"But how can they expect me to—"

"It's called acting, Coco," Haley reminded her.

"Maybe the script can be changed," Coco said.

"You can't change it." Haley stabbed the book with her finger. "It's right here in black and white."

"I can change it if I want to," Coco said emphatically. "Or there won't be a play."

Mr. Lyons, the drama teacher, clapped his hands and called for order. "All right, people! Let's keep things rolling. I'm still looking at Titanias. Let's see who's next." He glanced at his clipboard, opened his mouth, hesitated and then called, "Coco De Clerq."

"That's *moi*." Coco snatched up her script and sauntered over to the stage. "Hi, Mr. Lyons."

"Hello, Coco," Mr. Lyons said. "Would you please read Titania's scene with Oberon, act two, scene one? I'll read Oberon."

Coco flipped through her book until she found the part. " 'Titania and Oberon enter.' "

"Right. I'll read the stage directions," Mr. Lyons said. "Here I go. 'Ill met by moonlight, proud Titania.' "

Coco stood on the stage, her hand on her hip, staring at the book.

"That's your cue, Coco," Mr. Lyons said.

"Oh. Okay. 'Ill met by moonlight, proud Titania.' "

"That's my part. I just read it," Mr. Lyons said.

Haley sat down. The crowd in the auditorium had grown quiet. Everyone was watching. There was an electric feeling in the air that they were all about to witness a train wreck, and no one wanted to miss it.

"So you read the next line," Mr. Lyons prompted.

Coco cleared her throat. " 'What, jealous Oberon! Fairies, skip hence! I have forsworn his bed and company!' "

Haley glanced at her script. Were there really so

many exclamation points in Titania's speech? Turned out there weren't. So why was Coco shouting all her lines?

" 'Tarry, rash wanton: am not I thy lord?' " Mr. Lyons read.

" 'Then I must be thy lady!' " Coco screeched. " 'But I know when thou hast stolen away from fairy land! And in the shape of Corin sat all day! Playing on pipes of corn and versing love to amorous Phillida!' "

"Okay, uh, good, Coco." Mr. Lyons put down his book. "I think you have a real, uh, grasp of the dramatics here. Can I talk to you for a minute?" He beckoned her off the stage.

"Does this mean I get the part?" Coco walked toward him, beaming.

"Just let me speak with you for a minute, please," Mr. Lyons said.

Coco and Mr. Lyons huddled at the edge of the stage for a few minutes. All Haley could make out was a loud "What?" from Coco early on. A few minutes later, she strutted down the aisle toward Haley and Whitney.

"What happened, Coc?" Whitney said. "Did you get it?"

"Even better," Coco said. "He wants me to be his *assistant director*. He thinks I have a natural flair for storytelling."

Yeah, right, Haley thought, looking dubious.

"Assistant director? Wow, that's awesome!" Whitney exclaimed.

"Mr. Lyons says I'm too good an actress for a silly little school production," Coco explained. "And that he'll need my skills to help raise the level of the acting all around." She smiled smugly, as if she actually believed it—but Haley knew what was up. Mr. Lyons didn't want to lose his funding, and at the same time, he didn't want to direct a bomb.

"We have two more Titanias to audition, and then we'll move on to Puck, Bottom and the lovers," Mr. Lyons said. "Next up, Mary Fernandez?"

"You know what?" Whitney said. "I don't think I want to audition after all."

Typical, Haley thought. *If Coco's not going to act, her mini-me won't either.*

"Good thinking, Whit," Coco said. "As assistant director I'd never give you a decent part anyway. Besides, I think you'd be much better on costumes."

Whitney let the original insult slide. "That would be a lot more fun," she said, already thinking about fabrics.

"I'll tell Mr. Lyons at the end of auditions," Coco said, writing *Whitney=costumes* in a notebook. "What about you, Miller? Ready to throw in the towel yet?"

"No," Haley said. "I still want to audition. Just to see what happens."

"Your funeral," Coco said, shaking her head.

Haley had no idea how her audition would turn out. "I need a few minutes to concentrate and gather my thoughts," she told Coco and Whitney.

"Good luck," Whitney said genuinely.

Haley settled in the front row and watched the rest of the tryouts. Shaun mounted the stage in his donkey's head and brought the house down with his slapstick reading of his lines. Afterward, Irene quietly went to Mr. Lyons and asked to scratch her name off the audition list. "I'd rather help design the sets," she offered. Haley wondered if Irene had succumbed to stage fright. She certainly looked a little green.

"Excellent," Mr. Lyons told Irene. "We'll need skilled artists to create the Athens I'm envisioning."

As Haley watched, she noticed what worked and what didn't in various line readings. How speaking the unfamiliar Elizabethan lines naturally—but still with a dramatic flair—seemed to work best. Facing the audience, speaking clearly and moving around made an actor more interesting to watch than someone who just stood there like a wooden soldier, reading straight from the text.

Haley paid extra attention when Devon took the stage, auditioning for Lysander and Demetrius. Devon had always been a little on the quiet side, so Haley was surprised to see him stride across the boards with great confidence. Mr. Lyons asked him to read one of Demetrius's speeches for a second time. Devon took a breath, closed his eyes, then opened them and began to speak.

" 'O Helen, goddess, nymph, perfect, divine! To what, my love, shall I compare thine eyes? Crystal is muddy. O, how ripe in show thy lips, those kissing cherries, tempting grow! That pure congealed white, high Taurus' snow, fann'd with the eastern wind, turns to a crow when thou hold'st up thy hand: O, let me kiss this princess of pure white, this seal of bliss!' "

The sound of Devon's voice made Haley swoon. The words were so romantic, and he said them with such *passion* . . . She felt more determined than ever to win the part of Helena. Then, if Devon played Demetrius, he would say those beautiful words directly to her.

Sebastian tried out for Demetrius as well. He read the same speech as Devon, though it was a touch harder to understand through his accent. But he looked magnificent onstage, his body moving gracefully across the platform, his hair gleaming in the lights. *What if he got the part instead of Devon?* Haley thought idly. Playing opposite Sebastian wouldn't be the end of the world.

Haley went outside for some air and to focus while Mr. Lyons auditioned boys for the part of Puck, the mischievous fairy. When Haley finally returned to the auditorium, Mr. Lyons announced, "We're on our last Puck, so Hermias and Helenas, get ready, you're next. Okay, let me see Spencer Eton."

Haley heard Coco and Whitney, ten rows behind her, gasp in surprise. Haley was pretty shocked herself. Spencer sauntered up the aisle as if he were the opening nightclub act in Las Vegas, waving and doing the old point-and-shoot. No one was cheering, but somehow it looked as if Spencer heard the roar of the crowd, at least in his head.

"I am that merry wanderer of the night," Spencer read with surprising verve.

Maybe he would make a good Puck, Haley thought, *that is, if merry night-wandering is involved.*

"Interesting. Thank you, Spencer," Mr. Lyons said. "Okay, girls, let's see some spirited Helenas and Hermias."

Before long Mr. Lyons called Haley's name. She stood up, her stomach fluttering nervously, and walked up to the stage.

"Please read from act three, scene two, Helena's speech," Mr. Lyons said. "Whenever you're ready."

Haley remembered that scene. Helena, who loves Demetrius, thinks her friends are trying to trick her, to make her think Demetrius loves her when she believes he loves Hermia. She feels betrayed by her friends; she doesn't know whom to trust. It was a feeling Haley could relate to. She opened her script and read the lines.

" 'Injurious Hermia! Most ungrateful maid! Have you conspired, have you with these contrived to bait me with this foul derision? Is all the counsel that we two have shared, the sisters' vows, the hours that we have spent, when we have chid the hasty-footed time for parting us,—O, is it all forgot? All school-days' friendship, childhood innocence?' "

Haley found herself lost in the words, in the sad, betrayed loneliness of poor, unrequited Helena, and for a few minutes she forgot she was onstage in front of dozens of people, being judged on her acting. When the speech was finished, she looked up. The stage light was in her eyes, and she couldn't see the audience well, but she sensed how quiet they were. No shifting in their seats, no whispering or talking or murmuring of lines. They'd really listened.

"Very nice," Mr. Lyons said. "Thank you, Haley."

Haley stepped off the stage and the next Helena was called. Her bones were buzzing with excitement and her first taste of the thrill of the theater.

"You were awesome," Irene said as Haley walked past the auditorium seats. "Really good. You'll get a part for sure."

"Thanks," Haley said, still dazed.

Coco pursed her lips, shook her head and glanced at her clipboard. "Nice try," she said. "But don't quit your day job."

Suddenly, Haley wondered if the part was hers after all.

Surprise, surprise—we have an actress on our hands. Haley has discovered a new talent she didn't know she had. Is anything more exciting than that?

But is Haley's fate as an actress really in Coco's hands? If that's the case, Coco is right—Haley might as well give up now. Is she kidding herself? What about all her other activities—does she really have time to memorize lines on top of everything else?

And what about the boy situation? Both Sebastian and Devon tried out, but in Haley's opinion Devon was the better actor. If she wants face time with Sebastian, she might be better off watching him in the pool.

If you think Haley should listen to Coco and forget about the play, go to the SWIM MEET on page 124. If you think Haley would rather spend time honing her acting skills with Devon, go to page 142 (ACTING COACH). Finally, if you think Haley should believe in herself, in her newfound acting talent and in whatever spark of humanity still resides in Coco's heart-on-ice, send her to page 137 (CASTING CALL).

Fate plays funny tricks sometimes—you never can tell how things will turn out.

Playing devil's advocate only works if you're the devil.

"**B**ack for more, eh?" Alex Martin said, giving Haley a self-satisfied smile as she walked into Debate Team Central for her first official competition. "You must be a glutton for punishment."

"I can't resist a challenge," Haley retorted, wishing she'd come up with something more clever to say. Alex Martin was such a smug smarty-pants. Why did Haley have to find him so easy on the eyes? In an uptight, geeky-cute way, of course. But still, things would have been much easier if she'd been able to despise him in peace.

"A challenge. Right," Alex said, leading her to her seat next to Annie on the Hillsdale team's side of the room. "Our first competition is against Ridgewood. It doesn't get more challenging than that. Hope you can hack it."

"Don't worry about me," Haley said with more confidence than she felt. She surveyed the Ridgewood team across the podium. The debaters were seated in the order they'd speak, and Haley was second from the end, which meant she'd be debating the intense-looking Ridgewood girl in the dark red cardigan. The young woman's thick black hair was smoothed back in a ponytail; her dark bushy brows formed two sharp lines over her piercing blue eyes; she had a pointy nose and chin, angular cheekbones and ruby lipstick to match her sweater.

"Yikes," Annie whispered. "Looks like Alex matched you against Firemouth Francine for your very first debate. Tough break, kid."

"Firemouth Francine?" Haley said. The name seemed to fit, though Haley didn't like the sound of it.

"Francine Kendall," Annie explained. "She's Ridgewood's captain. A legend, and not just in her own mind. Her arguments are airtight and they sting. She makes her opponents look like morons. And she usually makes them cry. We've never beaten them, and it's because of her."

"Great." Haley cast an irritated glance at Alex, who took his seat beside her as last debater. He'd purposely given her the toughest competitor in the history of high school debating for her very first contest, in a mean-spirited attempt to break her and make her quit the team. Or so Haley had to assume.

"I thought you might need this," Alex said, straightening his red-and-blue-striped repp tie and handing Haley a handkerchief. "I suppose I'll be accepting your resignation by the end of the afternoon."

"Don't worry, you won't be seeing any tears out of these eyes," Haley said bravely.

"Oh, that's right," Alex said. "You're a tough girl. Maybe you ought to stick to the soccer field and leave the debate team to the intellects."

"Haven't you ever heard the term *well rounded*?" Haley snapped. "Some people can be athletic *and* intellectual."

"That's suburban myth," Alex said matter-of-factly. "A jock is a jock—and they're usually called dumb for a reason."

What an arrogant jerk! Haley tried to look unruffled as she sat in her seat, inwardly fuming at him. *So pretentious! And so full of himself! What has he ever done to demonstrate his fantastic intellect?*

"Alex, lay off her," Annie commanded.

"This is nothing," Alex said. "Just a warm-up. If she can't take a little ribbing she's in the wrong place."

Haley silently wondered if maybe he was right.

Ms. Dearborn, a history teacher and the debate team's faculty advisor, took the podium to begin the meet. "Welcome to Hillsdale High, Ridgewood debaters. This is our first meet of the year and it looks as if it could be one of the fiercest. So best of luck to you all. Our topic today: nature versus nurture. Resolved: the genes a child is born with have more effect on that child's life than the conditions in which he or she is raised. Ridgewood takes the pro side. We'll begin with Ridgewood's first debater, freshman Nancy Zewicki."

Haley listened carefully, making notes in the margins of her own argument, while Nancy Zewicki, a ditzy redhead in a fringed dress argued that a person's fate is set at birth, though not just because of genetics. "Just look at the ancient study of astrology," Nancy said without a hint of irony. "For centuries people have believed that the pattern of the stars you were born under decides the course of your life. Has anyone ever proven this theory wrong? I'm a Sagittarius myself, and every profile I've ever read totally, like so totally, fits me."

Nancy Zewicki—Ridgewood's version of Whitney Klein, Haley scribbled in her notebook. Annie glanced at the note, circled it and scrawled *so totally!* beside it.

"But don't be fooled," Annie whispered. "This is part of their strategy. They lull you into a false sense of superiority and then go in for the kill."

The next few Ridgewood debaters were tougher, just as Annie had predicted. Haley had a hard time concentrating on what they were saying. Her mind kept drifting to Alex and his obnoxious comments. How could he call her a dumb jock, after she practically blew him away at her debate tryout? Why was he so determined to put her down? Her heart was racing, but it wasn't simple nerves that stirred her blood—it was her growing wrath.

Annie nudged her. "Pay attention! Firemouth is up."

Francine Kendall stood at the podium with regal posture, clacking her note cards on the wood. "Nature versus nurture is the chicken-and-egg conundrum of modern science," she began. "The classic conflict. But scientists have made great strides recently in the study of genetics, and the more they learn, the stronger the evidence: your genes are your destiny. In 2003 a team of researchers at Oxford University began a rigorous blind study. . . ."

Oh, no, Haley thought. Firemouth had killer stats. She'd obviously spent hours in the library researching this topic. Haley would have liked to do more research, but who had the time?

"The identical twins were separated at birth and raised on two different continents," Francine was saying when Haley tuned back in. "They never knew of each other's existence. And yet both were good at spelling and bad at math, both became competitive springboard divers, and both developed tonsillitis at the age of seven. . . ."

Alex turned to Haley and waggled his eyebrows at her, as if to say, *Top that, jockette*. What was his problem? Didn't he want his own team to win?

The smoldering fury in Haley's chest raged to a full-blown inferno by the time Francine concluded her argument. Haley took the podium, hardly knowing what she was doing, barely glancing at her notes. She didn't need them. The argument poured out of her. She wasn't the daughter of two social justice fanatics for nothing. This was one argument she had down cold—and her anger at Alex seemed to ignite her brain.

"No one would argue that genetics are not important in any person's formation," Haley said. "But study after study has shown that children—even adopted children, who don't share their parents' genes—are most influenced by the behavior of those around them, particularly their parents. Abuse an adopted child, and that child will most likely grow up to be abusive, whether his birth parents were or not. Nurture is powerful enough to override nature in almost everything—even disease. Just look at the effects of behavioral elements like smoking or diet on health. . . ."

Haley was on fire. She could almost see the smoke coming out of her mouth as she spoke. *Who's the fire mouth now?* Haley thought as her words tumbled out so smoothly and articulately even she was a little surprised. When she was finished, both debate teams gaped at her, stunned.

Haley took her seat. "You killed it," Annie whispered. "Did you see the look on Francine's face?"

Alex cleared his throat and shifted uncomfortably in his chair as Ridgewood's final debater—a boy named Mark Deavers—made his argument. Then it was Alex's turn to speak. The judges took a few minutes to consult, then ruled in favor of Hillsdale, four–three. For the first time in five years, the Hawks had beaten Ridgewood.

Francine Kendall came over to shake Haley's hand personally. "Congratulations. You seem very passionate on this subject. It's always hard to defeat someone who really believes in what they're saying."

"Thank you," Haley said, though she wondered what she'd really been so passionate about. Was it really nature versus nurture? Or was it something else? Something to do with Alex Martin?

"Great job, Haley," Annie said. "You're an invaluable addition to the team. I'm so glad I overrode Alex on accepting you."

"Speaking of Alex . . . ," Haley said as Alex approached. She waited for him to apologize, to admit his dumb-jock characterization of her was way off base.

Instead he said, "You're welcome." And walked away.

You're welcome? You're welcome for what?

"Do you believe that guy?" Haley said to Annie. "He thinks I should thank him for pissing me off before the debate—is that it? Is he taking credit for our victory? For *my* performance? He's trying to say it was some sort of strategy?"

"Uh, it looks that way," Annie said. "And guess what—it worked."

Speechless, Haley walked through the school on her way to the bike rack. She couldn't stop thinking about Alex. She kept seeing his face in front of her, arching his eyebrows, smirking that smirk, and she didn't know whether to laugh or scream. So manipulative, so arrogant, so infuriating . . . and yet . . . so irresistible, too.

The debate had gone late and the school was now quiet, almost entirely empty for the day. Haley went out the back door of the building and spotted Irene and Devon carrying big cans of floor paint. *What are they up to?* Haley wondered. *Why are they even here at school at this hour?* Haley didn't want to think the worst, but this did look suspicious. Irene, after all, was no stranger to pranks. Shaun had grafittied her likeness on this very building just a year ago. And there was something dark and brooding about Devon. Haley considered whether to investigate.

● ● ●

The rebels are definitely known for their mischievous side. Irene and Devon are capable of just about anything, Haley is sure. Especially when it involves paint and the back of the school building. But is this something Haley should know more about?

And what about Alex Martin? He sure loves the head games. Is there another side to him—a less intellectual side? Could he be good at something besides mouthing off? Is he the least bit, as Haley mentioned, well rounded? After all, no one is all brain. He does have a body to go with that beautiful mind.

Haley's love life is pretty turbulent right now, with multiple guys swirling around her like satellites, and she has yet to really settle on one. If you think Alex has a hidden good side, send Haley home to think about her romantic prospects on page 150 (GUEST APPEARANCE).

Haley's nothing if not curious, and she's likely to wonder about Devon and Irene and their latest "art project" for some time. If you think Haley should follow them and find out what they're up to, go to page 173 (SET DESIGN).

Which is stronger, the head or the heart? Sounds like a good topic for another debate. Who will help Haley sort out the answer?

SWIM MEET

You can tread water
only so long.

"**A**re you going to the swim meet?" Haley asked
Reese as they left the math wing at the end of the
school day. "First of the season. I hear Zoe Jones is
trying out her new dive."

"Much as I would like to see her try that triple
back flip, I can't." Reese ran a hand through his dark
shaggy hair, leaving it looking perfectly mussed. The
jaw muscles in his chiseled face twitched slightly,
showing signs of strain. "I've got to go to the library

and research my paper for AP history. Plus SAT prep, plus soccer practice, plus everything else . . ."

"Oh," Haley said, not doing a particularly good job of hiding her disappointment. Reese had been so busy this fall, she felt as if she'd hardly seen him. All he ever seemed to do was study. He was totally caught up in the college treadmill. They all were, but Reese seemed to feel the pressure more than the rest. He was always good at everything, but now he had to be better than that. He had to be a total, all-around star. Haley didn't know what was keeping him going, or what was driving him so hard to be the best. But she had a feeling that drive was taking its toll, certainly on their relationship.

"See you tomorrow," Reese said, heading off to the library. He flashed her that irresistible grin and, for the moment, all was forgiven. Then Haley walked over to the swim center by herself.

A large crowd had already assembled by the time she got there. The pool was buzzing with excitement, shouts and whistles echoing off the tile walls. Haley spotted several unfamiliar adults peppered through the crowd and figured they were probably college recruiters, there to check out Sebastian and Haley's latest aquatics star, Zoe Jones.

The varsity boys lined up for the 100-meter butterfly, shaking their limbs to warm up. It was hard to miss Sebastian in lane three. He'd grown over the summer, if that was even possible, and now his broad shoulders rippled with even more and leaner muscles. It was also hard to miss his biggest fan in the front row, clapping and shouting, "Sebastian, olé! Bravo!" In fact, every eye in the swim center was drawn to the tall, glamorous Mia Delgado, and she certainly didn't seem to mind the attention. She was surrounded by admiring boys, who seemed to be oblivious to the fact that she was cheering for her supposed boyfriend.

Sebastian turned toward the crowd, grinned and waved at Mia, then resumed his warm-up. Haley looked for Coco De Clerq, Sasha Lewis or Whitney Klein, but didn't see any of them, so she took a seat in the top row of bleachers, as far from the Mia attention-vortex as she could get.

Sebastian won the 100-meter butterfly easily, blowing his competition out of the water, so to speak. "Woo-hoo! *Magnífico,* Sebastian!" Mia cheered.

Just before the next race, Coco walked in, trailed by her once again constant shadow, Whitney. Whitney noticed Haley in the stands and waved enthusiastically, nudging Coco in her direction. Haley moved over to make room for the dramatic duo, but Coco only flapped her hand at Haley before beelining to front-row center, where Mia was holding court.

Humph, Haley thought, stung, as she watched Coco shove her way into the seat next to Mia, exchange triple air-kisses and coo over the low-cut jersey top Mia was wearing. It looked as if Coco was back to living by her old motto: "Keep your friends close and the new pretty girl closer."

Haley felt a knot of jealousy tighten in her stomach. There she was, sitting all alone in the stands while the populettes dominated the front row, ignoring her. Haley had been at Hillsdale for over a year now; she thought she had the place figured out. She had at least a few friends now. At times she'd even ruled the school. But suddenly she was transported back to the miserable early days of her sophomore year, when she was the lonliest girl in the room.

The buzzer sounded and the 200-meter freestyle, Sebastian's specialty, began. He dove into the water and pulled ahead from the beginning. Haley stood up to watch. This was what she'd come for, after all. Sebastian looked fantastic, his strokes smooth and powerful, and he easily won this race too. Mia screamed with excitement, jumping up and down and whipping her long dark hair around. Coco clapped and hugged Mia as if they were lifelong BFFs. The guys surrounding the Spanish beauty jumped in for hugs too, and she gladly embraced anybody who came within two feet of her, babbling happily in Spanish. The recruiters, too, looked very impressed.

Sebastian waved to the crowd, blew another kiss to Mia and left the pool to stretch before his next race. Meanwhile, the varsity girls had lined up for a relay. Haley opened her calculus book and glanced at a few homework problems. She felt like the biggest geek in the world, but what else was she going to do? It was not as if she had any friends to chat with. Reese was gone, studying at the library. And Sebastian didn't appear to be acknowledging she was alive.

The race starter buzzed again, and Haley looked up from her book to watch the girls' relay, but she was distracted by the sight of the pool door opening. Alex Martin walked in. He glanced at the girls in the water, then checked the stands. When he spotted Haley, he waved and walked straight over to her.

Haley braced herself. She didn't know much about Alex, except that he was a senior and cocaptain of the debate team, and that he was intense. Talking to him certainly kept her on her toes. She couldn't help noticing, as she watched him climb the bleachers, that in spite of his intensity he looked adorable. His usually impeccable short chestnut hair was slightly askew, and his preppy clothes had rumpled a bit over the course of the day, making him seem warmer, less formal and intimidating.

"Hey, Haley," he said, sitting beside her. "You've got the best seat in the house."

Haley surveyed the empty seats around them. "You know what they say—it's lonely at the top."

Alex laughed, a surprisingly easy chuckle, and Haley realized there was a lot to Alex that she hadn't anticipated.

Down at the pool, the boys lined up for the

freestyle sprints, and there was Sebastian again, swinging his long arms from side to side. "*Vámonos, Sebastian, let's go!*" Mia shouted in her husky voice.

"Go Sebastian!" Coco and Whitney echoed. Mia put her arms around them and the curvy trio bounced up and down, much to the delight of all the boys around them. The girls were suddenly the best of friends. What did they need Haley for?

"The team looks excellent this year, don't they?" Alex said. Haley was relieved to have a distraction from the cheering squad below. "I hear Sebastian is an Olympic-level swimmer."

"He is pretty awesome," Haley said. "Though unfortunately, he knows it. Just watch this sprint."

The starter buzzed and the swimmers were off. Once again, Sebastian glided through the water, fishlike, and won with little competition.

"I guess some people are just born comfortable in the water," Alex said, attempting to strike up conversation. "Not me. My parents had to bribe me with a saxophone to get me to learn how to swim."

Haley smiled. "What's your element, then?" she asked.

Alex thought for a minute. "Good question. Definitely not air—I'm afraid of heights and get nervous on planes. And not fire—whose element is fire, anyway?"

"Chefs?" Haley offered.

"Interesting," Alex said.

"That really only leaves earth for you," Haley replied.

"Do books qualify as earth?" Alex asked. "That's my real element, if you ask me."

Haley was impressed with how well he knew himself.

"And where are you most comfortable, Haley Miller?"

"Good question," Haley said. What *was* her element? She sometimes felt like she hadn't a clue.

● ● ●

Talking to Alex must be kind of refreshing for Haley. He's so different from the other boys at Hillsdale. And once you chill him out a degree or twenty, he could actually be . . . kind of appealing.

But what exactly is he doing at the swim meet? He's clearly no sports fan. Did he go there looking for Haley? He sure seemed eager to sit with her.

And if he *is* flirting with her, how does Haley feel about it? And what will Reese think? Here Reese is, slaving away alone in the library. And Haley's off discussing the elements of life with Alex? If she found Reese in a similar situation with a girl, wouldn't she be jealous?

On the other hand, Reese has been paying more attention to his books than to Haley lately, so maybe he's lost all claim to her. You can't leave a cute girl like Haley alone for long before someone else tries to fill the empty seat. Reese knows that, or else he should.

Speaking of jealousy, what's up with Coco? Since when are she and Mia Delgado the best of friends? Is Coco just using Mia, trying to siphon away some of that male attention? Or is Mia using Coco to increase her social power? Anything's possible with those two.

If you think Haley should keep the door open for new boys, turn to page 150 (GUEST APPEARANCE). If you think she's more intrigued by Coco and Mia's new friendship and what's behind it, get to know Mia better on page 157 (FIRE AND ICE). Finally, if you think Haley's had enough of Coco, Mia and Alex, and wishes she were hanging with the easygoing Sasha instead, go to page 166 (BUYER'S REMORSE).

What is Haley's natural element? It's up to you to help her find it.

FANCY FOOTWORK

Sometimes politeness can feel like a slap in the face.

"Okay, Hawks." Cocaptains Haley and Sasha gathered the soccer team in a pregame huddle. The girls piled their hands in the center of the circle. "Ooooooh let's go!" they chanted, clapping, revved up for their first home game of the season.

"Let's start the year out right, everybody," Sasha said as they ran onto the field. It was a crisp fall afternoon. Haley pumped her legs and arms to warm them up. "Go Hawks!" a trio of freshmen shouted from the sidelines. The stands were full, especially since the boys' varsity team lined the front row. They had their first home game that day too, after the girls played. Knowing the boys were watching psyched up the girls even more.

"Forward momentum, girls!" Coach Tygert called out as they took their positions. "Stay on your toes!"

Haley glanced at the spectators just before the ref blew her whistle to start the game. Reese sat at the end of the front row in his soccer uniform, his dark hair gleaming in the sun. He flashed her a smile and waved, and Haley's face flushed happily. Reese really was perfect boyfriend material. He and Haley shared so much in common: they worked hard in school but could play hard too—whether on the soccer field or with friends. Plus, they even lived next door to each other. How cosmic was that?

The whistle blew, play started and Haley lost herself in the game. Sasha immediately cornered the ball and, with her long legs, dribbled it up the field toward the North Bergen goal. She aimed a long, graceful kick at the net, but the North Bergen goalie blocked it.

"Good hustle, Sash!" Haley called as they went on defense. The Hawks blocked several attacks at their goal, and perky sophomore Christina Schindler made a nice pass to Sasha, who scored one for Hillsdale. North Bergen came back to tie the game just before the ref blew the whistle to end the first half.

"You're looking good out there, girls," Coach

Tygert said. "But let's be more aggressive. Their goalie's shaky—keep shooting and we'll score again."

Haley waved to Reese as she returned to the field for the second half, but he didn't see. He had his head down and was hastily scribbling in a workbook now, apparently too focused on solving math problems to watch Haley play. *He'll look up once the whistle blows,* Haley told herself.

The second half plodded along with no score on either side. It seemed as though Hillsdale might have to settle for a tie, if North Bergen didn't manage to score on them by game's end. With only a few minutes left on the clock, Haley intercepted the ball and found herself mere feet from the goal, with most of North Bergen's defense behind her. She arced the ball toward the net . . . the goalie jumped, missed and the ball went in!

"All right, Haley!" her teammates squealed, jumping on top of her and hugging each other. "Two–one Hillsdale!"

"Nice job, Miller," Coach Tygert shouted.

Sasha patted her on the back. "Way to win the game, superstar."

As she jogged back to her position, Haley glanced into the stands to get her usual thumbs-up from Reese. But he wasn't even looking at the field— his head was still buried in a thick textbook.

He hadn't seen her goal.

One of his teammates saw Haley staring and nudged Reese, then pointed in her direction. Reese looked up from his book and waved absently.

Too late, Haley thought. *I already caught you not looking.*

Haley was distracted for the rest of the game. She played fine, even blocked a last-ditch North Bergen sideline kick for a steal. But every time she checked the stands, Reese wasn't paying attention. *Why does he even bother to sit there?* she wondered. It was just a charade. He might as well be in the library for all he cared about the game. Maybe Reese Highland wasn't such perfect boyfriend material after all.

Hillsdale won, 2–1, thanks to Haley's goal, and as she jogged off the field, passing the bleachers on her way to the locker room, Reese reached for her hand with a half shake. "That goal was, um, a beauty," he said sheepishly.

"Thanks," Haley said. But what she was thinking was, *How would you know? You didn't even see it, you liar.*

"I'd better start warming up," Reese said as he and his teammates jogged onto the field. "Are you going to stay and watch our game?"

"I can't," Haley said. "I've got too much *homework*." She turned and jogged off to the locker room to take a hot shower, and celebrate the win with the rest of her team.

• • •

Are Reese and Haley in trouble? Reese is so focused on school and extracurriculars right now that he's totally neglecting his girl. He barely watched Haley's game, completely missed her all-important goal, yet he expects her to stay and cheer for him? Not likely.

Okay, so it's fall semester junior year, a pretty stressful time for any high school student. But is that really any excuse? If Reese neglects Haley to pad his college applications, what does that mean for their love life down the road? Will this go on all year? Or will Reese eventually find his way back to her? Should Haley put up with it, or does she deserve better? After all, she's pretty busy herself. Maybe a part-time boyfriend makes sense.

What should Haley do now? Maybe she needs to go home and think about the relationship and where it's headed. To send her home to mull over Reese's behavior, go to page 150 (GUEST APPEARANCE). Or perhaps what Haley needs is to clear her head with some quality girl time. To have her stick with Sasha after the game, go to page 166 (BUYER'S REMORSE).

Looks as if dating Reese does have a downside. Sadly, no one's flawless. Not even Reese.

CASTING CALL

Take the lead, follow
or get out of the play.

"Haley, come here." Coco waved Haley over to a bench in the rotunda. Haley had time to kill between classes, so she obliged. "I've got news you'll be interested in—the cast list is official!"

"So did I get a part?" Haley asked.

"I'll tell you in a minute," Coco said.

Typical, Haley thought. *She has to lord it over me until the last possible minute.*

As assistant director, Coco was reveling in her power over her actors' fragile egos. "First I have to call all the losers who didn't get parts and break the bad news to them," Coco enthused.

"Won't they find out when you post the cast list?" Haley said.

"Sure, but this is sooo much more fun." Coco flicked open her cell phone and started punching numbers.

"But what about me?" Haley practically screamed.

"Chillax, Miller," Coco said dismissively. "You'll find out your fate soon enough. Hello, is this Candy Davenport? Hi, this is Coco De Clerq, the director of the fall play?"

"Assistant director," Haley corrected.

"Shhh." Coco covered the phone and hissed at Haley. "Anyway, we've settled on the cast list and I thought you'd be anxious to hear—"

Even from where she was sitting Haley could hear Candy's excited screams. "I got the lead? I got the lead?"

"No, sorry, Candy darling, you didn't get the lead," Coco said. "You didn't get any part at all. Not even a nameless fairy just standing around in the background flapping her wings. Nope, nothing. I knew you'd want to know right away. So that you don't waste any more of your time fantasizing about an acting career. Thanks so much for auditioning. Maybe next year. Buh-bye!"

"Coco, that was so mean," Haley said as Coco dialed the next number.

"I know, wasn't it? But if you think about it, I'm being considerate, not keeping them in suspense—Hello, Tessa?"

Haley fidgeted as she waited for Coco to finish running through her list of "Sorry, you lose" calls. Had she gotten a part or not? She really wanted to play Helena, but Hermia would be great too. She tried to sneak a peek at the cast list, but Coco kept it covered in her burgundy leather bag.

"Fine, I'm leaving if you're not going to show me that cast list." Haley was seething.

"Oh, all right," Coco said as Haley was about to storm off. "You'll be the lucky girl who gets the good news first. But don't tell anyone—I want the chance to tell the others myself."

"Okay, okay! Just tell me!"

"Haley, I'm happy to inform you that you will be playing the part of . . . Helena."

Haley sighed with relief. "That's fantastic! Now, who's playing Demetrius?"

Coco took a long pause, deliberating on whether or not to reveal the choice to Haley. "Devon McKnight," Coco said finally. "Not my first choice, but what are you going to do." She scanned the list for the highlights. "Let's see . . . Spencer's playing Puck, of course—I think he'll be fabulous, don't you?"

"If you say so," Haley agreed.

"And Shaun is playing Nick Bottom." Coco made a face. "Against my wishes, but Mr. Lyons insisted. I think the fact that he auditioned wearing an ass's head sealed the deal."

"Shaun was really funny in his tryout, you have to admit," Haley offered.

"I admit nothing."

"Who's playing Titania?" Haley asked, wondering who would get the most coveted role in the play.

"Mia, of course," Coco said. "Titania has to be a regal beauty. And there aren't too many of those in this school. Present company excepted, of course."

"Of course." Haley knew she meant that the exception was Coco, not Haley.

"I would have been a dynamite Titania, but my talents were needed elsewhere," Coco said. "I'm happy to make the sacrifice."

"We're all thrilled too," Haley said. Nothing Coco said could bother her now—she was too excited. She'd gotten Helena! And Helena would have her Demetrius, meaning Haley was about to start seeing an awful lot of Devon.

● ● ●

Awesome news! Haley got the part she wanted, and Devon will be her love interest. But will the romance continue offstage? This is a fascinating development that could change the course of Haley's love—and social—life for the rest of the year. The play is a big production involving all kinds of kids, from the popular Cocobots to the geeky stage crew and the artsy set designers. As part of the theater crowd, Haley can move in so many different directions.

If you think she should stay on Assistant Director Coco's good side and spend more time with the beautiful people, go to page 157 (FIRE AND ICE). If you think hanging with Devon, Irene and Shaun will have a better effect on Haley's acting ability, go to page 173 (SET DESIGN).

The stage is set, the players chosen. Now let the drama begin!

There's Method
in this madness.

"CONGRATULATIONTH, my petth!" Xavier Willkommen, tutor extraordinaire, exclaimed as he grandly swept into his cousin Shaun's living room. As usual, he was ridiculously dressed in a lavender shirt with pearly buttons, a yellow paisley ascot and a black tuxedo jacket. With tails. "My teachingth have been thuthethful beyond even my WILDETHT expectationth. Ath I underthtand it, in thith very room we have three—count, them, THREE—newly minted thtage ACTORTH!"

"And one cowardly stage designer," Irene offered, raising her hand.

"Nonthense, dearetht," Xavier said. "Thtage design ith an ART in and of itthelf. Tho ith knowing where your true talentth lie. And Devon, you'll be working both thideth of the thtage, I hear."

Devon was both playing Demetrius and helping Irene paint the sets. Haley had gotten the part of Helena, a girl who loves Demetrius but is not loved back (until the happy ending, of course), and Shaun landed his dream role of Nick Bottom, the weaver-victim of a fairy's spell, which turns his head into an ass's.

"Dude, I wore a papier-mâché donkey head to the audition, and it totally paid off," Shaun told Xavier. "Way to channel the Method, am I right?"

"Thatth a good beginning, Thhaun," Xavier said. "Why don't we thpend part of each tutoring thethion from here on rehearthing your lineth? If you don't mind, Irene. Even though you won't be acting in the play, we can all learn thomething about the human THPIRIT from the CLATHIC acting techniques. Letth begin with thome exerthitheth developed by the GREAT and POWERFUL Thanford Meithner."

Xavier told Shaun and Irene to stand in front of the group, facing each other. Shaun impulsively leaned over and kissed Irene's nose.

Irene jumped back, rubbing her wet face. "Ew. Shaun, no PDA during tutoring."

"Irene ith correct," Xavier said. "One of Meithner'th ruleth ith NO TOUCHING. You have to convey everything with your VOITHE. Now. Thith exerthithe ith called repetithion. Thhaun, look around the room and make a one-thententhe obthervathion about thomething you thee. Then, Irene, you repeat what he thayth ath a quethtion. Thhaun, you repeat the obthervathion, emphathithing a different word each time. Ready? Go."

Shaun looked around until his eyes fell upon one of his favorite things, a banana, resting on the kitchen counter. "What a beautiful yellow banana," Shaun said.

"Look Irene directly in the eye the whole time," Xavier said.

Shaun looked Irene in the eye. "What a beautiful yellow banana."

"What a beautiful yellow banana?" Irene said.

"What a BEAUTIFUL yellow banana," Shaun said.

"What a BEAUTIFUL yellow banana?" Irene said.

"Good," Xavier said. "FEED off each otherth emothionth."

"What a beautiful YELLOW banana," Shaun said.

"What a beautiful YELLOW banana?" Irene said.

"WHAT a beautiful yellow banana," Shaun said.

"WHAT a stupid-ass boring exercise?" Irene said.

"No, no, no, NO." Xavier rose to his feet. "Thtay in the moment, Irene. I know it feelth thilly at firtht, but we're learning that one change in your inflec-thion can COMPLETELY alter the meaning of a line. Thith ith ethpethially important with Thhakespeare, my petth. Devon and Haley, your turn."

Haley stood up, looked Devon in the eye and re-peated every possible permutation of "You have a hole in the knee of your jeans" until the subject of knee holes was exhausted.

"Good," Xavier said. "Okay. You're thtarting to get the githt of it. Letth move on to Uta Hagenth protheth. Hagen and Meithner are both offthhootth of the Thtanithlavthky Method, developed in New York by Lee Thtrathberg. The idea behind the Method is that you draw on your own emothionth and experientheth to find a way to portray your character convinthingly. Uta Hagen took that farther by thaying that ACTHION ith TRUTH. We are ACTORTH, not FEELERTH. We DO. The thimple ith PROFOUND. Be TRUTHFUL in the THIMPLE."

"Dude, WHAT are you talking about?" Shaun said.

"Your character hath the head of a donkey," Xavier said. "Now, you may not have any experien-the being a donkey. But if you act like an ath all the time, you will begin to know what it feelth like to BE an ath. You will BECOME the ath. And that will make your character convinthing to the audienthe."

Shaun's face lit up. Irene held her head in her hands. "Oh no," she groaned. "He gets it."

"I totally get it now," Shaun said. "*Hee-haw, hee-haw!* I've got to live like a donkey all the time! Awesome."

"Just until the play is over," Devon said.

"Please," Irene said. "Don't encourage this. Xavier, you don't mean he has to literally be an ass? I mean, even more than usual?"

Xavier frowned thoughtfully. "Well, it doeth kind of mean that. Like when Robert De Niro gained thickthty poundth to play Jake La Motta for *Raging Bull*. You've got to phythically BE the character, and cothtumes alone aren't enough."

"This is going to be a nightmare," Irene said.

"Maybe not," Haley said. "I mean, if you think about it . . . Shaun pretending to be an ass, Shaun acting normally . . . what's the difference, really?"

"Right on, Haley," Shaun said.

"Shaun, she just insulted you," Irene said. "Not that I blame her."

"Oh," Shaun said. "Well, hee-haw. I'm an ass. I don't get insulted."

"Good, Thhaun," Xavier said. "You're really LIV-ING Nick Bottom."

"Damn right I am," Shaun said.

"Letth try another exerthithe," Xavier said. "Haley, your character, Helena, ith pathionately in love, but itth unrequited. I want you to thhow me Helena in love. Dig deep into your own feelingth,

146

your patht experientheth, and find a way to TH-HOW me that feeling."

Haley hesitated. "This is getting pretty personal."

"Exactly," Xavier said. "Thatth what we WANT. Think of thomeone you love and find a way to expreth that feeling tho we'll all thee it."

Haley liked the idea of channeling her character through her own life. It made sense to her, and she knew it was the only way she'd be able to pull off a major role onstage. Without that technique she was afraid she'd be wooden. But there was one problem: she had to think of someone she loved passionately, the way Helena loved Demetrius. Whom, if anyone, did she love that much?

"You can trutht uth with your deepetht feelingth, Haley," Xavier said. "We're your friendth. RELAX into trutht."

Haley looked at the faces of Irene, Shaun and Devon. She did trust them. It wasn't that.

Had she ever been passionately in love? Was she now?

If so, with whom? Devon was playing Demetrius. Maybe he was the perfect person to think about.

But maybe not. PASSIONATELY in love? That wasn't the right word for her feelings for Devon. Not yet, anyway.

"I'm still having trouble," Haley said.

"Think of thomeone who, if he died, you'd be

CRUTHHED," Xavier said. "Who ith that perthon in your life?"

Suddenly a face appeared in Haley's mind. Just thinking about that face, thinking of him dying, nearly brought her to tears. Her eyes actually got misty when she thought about him.

That was it. He was the one. The key to Haley's deepest emotions.

"I'm thtarting to thee it," Xavier said. "Everyone, do you thee the tenderneth in her eyeth? Thay thomething, Haley. Tell uth how you feel."

"Oh Freckles!" Haley cried. "I love you so much!"

Devon and Irene laughed. "Freckles?" Irene said. "Your dog?"

"It ith not for uth to JUDGE, people," Xavier said. "Thethe choitheth are HIGHLY perthonal." But Haley thought she saw him stifling a laugh too.

"I don't think it's funny," Shaun said. "I mean, I'm an ass. An animal, like Freckles. I can only hope the beautiful Queen Titania will feel about me the way Haley feels about Freckles." Shaun began to tear up.

"Amen, Thhaun," Xavier said. "My loveth, today we've theen the birth of an actor."

● ● ●

Haley is starting to get the hang of this acting business, even if some of Xavier's methods seem silly at first. It's all pretty intense, though. If you think Haley could use

a break from the theater crowd and would find an afternoon with Sasha refreshing, go to page 166 (BUYER'S REMORSE). If you'd like Haley to stick with her fellow artistes, go to page 173 (SET DESIGN).

For serious theater people, acting is a calling, not a hobby. The question is, is it calling out to Haley?

GUEST APPEARANCE

Resolved: if you can't be with the one you love, love the one you're with. Discuss.

"Mitchell, get the door!" Haley called downstairs. Her parents were out, and Mitchell was in the basement, most likely destroying something. Haley was up in her room doing practice SAT math problems. At least, she was supposed to be doing math problems. Her mind was actually more focused on romantic problems—like Reese Highland's recent disappearing act.

"You get it," Mitchell called back. "I'm busy disassembling the remote."

Right again, Haley thought. She put down her pencil and walked downstairs as the doorbell rang a second time. "Coming!" she called. "Mitchell, you'd better be able to put that remote back together before Mom and Dad get home." Perry could get pretty cranky if he couldn't pause, slow-mo or resee scenes in his favorite films.

"Don't worry," Mitchell said. "I have complete faith in myself."

That's for sure, Haley thought. And it was true that so far Mitchell had been able to reassemble everything he'd meticulously broken down, including her camera, which had stopped sticking between frames and now worked better than it did before.

Haley peeked through the window next to the heavy front door and gasped at the sight of Alex Martin. He stood patiently on her front porch in his belted khakis and a polo shirt, his short chestnut hair neatly combed.

What was *he* doing here? What could he possibly want?

Haley racked her brain for any memory of invitations to her house—study groups, debate team meetings she might have volunteered to host—but came up blank.

There's only one way to find out, a little voice in Haley's head said. *Open the door, stupid.*

"Hi, Alex," she said, leaning against the doorframe.

"Hello, Haley. I was in the neighborhood and thought I'd stop by."

In the neighborhood? Please.

"Um, great," Haley said. She stood there waiting to hear what he wanted, but he seemed to be ceding the floor to her. Talk about awkward.

"I was wondering if you'd like to go out for some frozen yogurt," Alex said at last.

Haley stepped out onto the porch. Alex's car, a shiny, expensive-looking black sedan, was parked in the driveway, ready to whisk her off for fro-yo. Meanwhile, the Highlands' house next door, Haley couldn't help noticing, looked completely empty. "Sorry, I can't," Haley said. "I'm watching my little brother."

"Oh," Alex said. She thought he'd leave then, but he didn't. He just seemed to be staring at the polish on his tassled brown loafers.

How arrogant of him to think he can just show up like this, Haley thought. Arrogant but flattering.

"But—well, if you want to sit on the porch and hang for a little while, that would be cool," Haley said. "We don't have any frozen yogurt, or even ice cream. My parents are pretty severely antisugar. But we could have some iced tea."

"Great," Alex said. "That would be just great."

Alex sat on the front porch while Haley went into the kitchen to fetch some glasses. She poured the unsweetened hibiscus tea over ice and brought the glasses outside with a plate of cheese and crackers.

"So—no sugar in the house," Alex said, taking a cracker. "Makes sense, given your other political views. Let me guess, your parents are old hippies. Fits with your geographical roots."

"My geographical roots?" Haley wasn't sure what he was talking about.

"Annie told me you moved here from Northern California. That explains the progressive stance, the granola nutrition, the obsession with the environment . . . it all fits."

"You've got me all figured out, don't you?" Haley said sarcastically. "Reduced to a Marin County stereotype."

Alex looked at her. "I'm sorry—you're right. People are a lot more complicated than we think. Especially people like you."

"People like me?" Haley said. "Don't you mean hippie spawn from San Francisco?"

"No. I mean smart people. People who think for themselves, even in the suffocatingly conformist environment of high school."

Her annoyance at being so neatly summed up now faded. Maybe Alex wasn't as obtuse as she'd thought. "What about you?" she asked. "What are *your* geographical roots?"

"Connecticut born. New Jersey bred," Alex said.

"My father moved his company here when I was three. Cheaper overhead. But I've managed to get out and see a little of the world. I spent last summer building houses for the poor in Costa Rica."

"*You?*" Somehow the idea of helping people in Central America didn't fit with Haley's image of Alex as staunch conservative capitalist pig. A cute capitalist pig, but then she'd always thought piglets were adorable. "I wouldn't have expected that."

"People are a lot more complicated than we think," Alex reminded her.

Haley began to relax, and they fell into a long conversation, oblivious to the time passing by. Haley soon realized it was getting dark out. She and Alex must have talked for over an hour. He was smart, intimidatingly so. Most of the kids Haley knew couldn't see past their little Hillsdale High bubble. She'd be shocked if they thought of anything outside the borders of Bergen County. Even the rich kids like Coco and Whitney shuttled from Hillsdale to the city to the Hamptons, with maybe a stop in Paris or London during breaks. But, even so, all they cared about was Hillsdale. This was their power base.

"I should probably get going," Alex said, standing up. Haley walked him to his car and saw that the Highlands' wagon was now parked in the driveway. She'd been so wrapped up in conversation with Alex she hadn't noticed anyone pull up. *Had Reese come home?* Haley wondered. *And if he had, had he seen her on the porch with Alex?*

What would Reese do if he *had* seen them? Would he come over to say hello? Be jealous that she was talking to another boy? Or not think much of it and leave them alone?

Haley wasn't sure.

"Thanks again for the iced tea," Alex said. "See you at school."

"Yeah. See you." Haley waved absently as he drove off, relieved that her mother wasn't around to see his gas-guzzling luxury car.

Later that evening, while working on the third draft of her college application essay, Haley got an Instant Message from Reese.

R: What's up, Red? Feels like it's been ages. Wanna meet me in the library tomorrow?

Without thinking, Haley typed back:

H: Sure. CU then.

She logged off and went back to her essay, but something about Reese's message bothered her. He'd been so busy studying lately, he hardly seemed to notice she was alive. Now all of a sudden he wanted to study with *her*?

Maybe he did see me with Alex, she thought.

Maybe he sensed that other boys are buzzing around, and he wants to remind me that I'm his.

But if he wanted to stake his claim, this was a lame way of doing it. Going to the library? What kind of date was that?

A sucky date, that's what.

● ● ●

Haley has a lot of options right now. Both Alex and Reese are nice guys—smart, well mannered and let's not forget hot. How to choose between Mr. Best All-around and Mr. Brainiac? Should Haley pick the one who seems more into her? That would have to be Alex—for the moment. But who knows—maybe once she agrees to go out with him he'll start ignoring her too, just like Reese. Boys are mysterious creatures.

If you think Haley should meet Reese at the library as planned, go to page 196 (SOLVING FOR EX). If you think she should bust out of her rut, put a little distance between herself and Reese Highland and live a little, go to page 200 (FREEDOM ROCK). If you think Haley should stop thinking about boys so much and focus on the college race, go to page 180 (SCATTERBRAINED).

Watch out. In the realm of love, you won't get explanations for certain unexpected twists of fate.

Some say the world will end in fire, some say in ice. And some say it will end in a hail of malicious gossip.

"I see Mia in something very royal, say, a velvet robe with gold trim," Coco said as she took her seat at a window table at Bubbies. Whitney sat next to her, with Haley and Cecily and Mia Delgado rounding out the circle. Coco had called the brunch meeting to discuss, among other things, the costumes for the school play, which were being designed by Whitney this year. The production was of Shakespeare's comedy *A Midsummer Night's Dream*. Coco, of course, was the assistant director, and Mia the star, though she already looked bored and they had been sitting at the table for only five minutes.

Mia was used to the little cafés and restaurants of Europe. Bubbies was a bistro in the European style, which meant it had rattan outdoor chairs and a Tuscan-Alpine-Provençal mural on the wall leading to the men's and women's restrooms. It was a favorite Hillsdale Heights spot for brunch, and being seen in the window on Sunday afternoon was a status symbol, like being seen on the deck of the country club or getting spotted with an armload of shopping bags near the downtown boutiques.

"I no like blue," Mia said, pouting. "It is a bad color for me."

"Mia's character is a fairy," Whitney said. "I was thinking of something more along the lines of a long, airy chiffon gown belted with gold."

"This sounds much better," Mia replied. "The chiffon, it is nice on my"—and here she looked dismissively at the other girls—"curves."

Coco sniffed. "I'm the director—"

"Assistant director," Cecily reminded her.

Coco ignored her. "—and I say Mia gets dressed in velvet. Royal blue. High neck. Empire waist. Stiff bodice."

"What about Mr. Lyons?" Whitney whispered. "He told me he wanted Titania in chiffon."

"I'll handle him," Coco commanded.

They scanned the menus and kept quiet for a few minutes, until Whitney finally whispered, "Oh my god, girls. Look who it is."

As if on cue, there was a loud crash, the sound of dishes shattering. Haley looked toward the kitchen and saw that Johnny Lane, Sasha's slick rocker boyfriend, had just dropped a plastic tub full of plates.

"I didn't know he worked here," Cecily said, which was surprising. Of everyone at the table, Cecily probably spent the most time with Sasha these days, and by extension, Johnny Lane.

Coco shrugged. "What do you expect? He's got to earn his drug money somewhere."

Whitney frowned. "I thought he earned his drug money selling drugs."

Just then, the waitress arrived to take their orders. "I'll have the Cobb salad, dressing on the side, and a diet soda," Coco said.

"I'd like the grilled chicken sandwich," Haley said. "And iced tea."

"Western omelet for me, please," Cecily ordered. "And lemonade."

"I'd like an omelet too," Mia said. "And *un café con leche.*"

"I'll have the bacon cheeseburger, medium rare," Whitney said. "With blue cheese. And fries, and a milk shake."

Coco shook her head. "No she won't. She'll have the Caesar salad with grilled chicken on top and a diet soda. Right, Whit?"

"I'm starving, Coco," Whitney said. "I haven't eaten since last night."

"This is brunch, Whitney," Coco said. "None of us have eaten since last night."

"Okay," Whitney said. "But I'm getting dessert."

"Whatever," Coco said, handing the waitress her menu.

A few seconds later Johnny arrived to fill their water glasses. He wasn't used to serving his classmates, so he acted gruff to cover up his embarrassment.

"Hi, Johnny," Cecily said, trying to act as if he weren't mopping up spilled water on the tablecloth in front of her.

"What's up?" Haley said, also attempting to make this humiliating moment easier on the guy.

"Hellllo," Mia purred, tracing her finger around the edge of her water glass. She took a sip, then let a piece of ice slip into her mouth.

Johnny looked at her, smirked and sauntered away, still cool even with an apron wrapped over his jeans and Clash T-shirt.

"Ohmigosh, how could Sasha do it with that guy?" Whitney whispered as soon as he was out of earshot.

"What do you mean, 'do it'?" Mia asked. "And who is Sasha?"

"You haven't met her yet?" Cecily asked. "Just

wait." Haley knew exactly what Cecily meant. Mia squaring off against Sasha in competition for a guy would be about the most evenly matched pairing Mia would come across at Hillsdale High. The sporty golden girl Sasha had all the fun and warmth Mia lacked, while Mia's smoldering, dangerous appeal made even the rebellious Sasha seem safe.

"Johnny and Sasha went camping in Virginia this summer and totally went all the way. In a pup tent," Whitney dished.

"That's such old news," Coco said.

"I wouldn't go spreading rumors, Whitney," Cecily added. "That's not quite how their little camping trip went."

Mia rolled her eyes. "You Americans are so hung up on sex. What is the big deal? She likes him, he likes her . . . it's the nature."

"What about you and Sebastian?" Whitney asked. "Have you . . . you know . . . ?"

Haley tensed slightly, waiting for the answer, but Mia laughed it off, as if to say, *Of course we have,* amiga.

"You want to know the real story?" Coco said, arching an eyebrow. "Sasha and Johnny almost did it, but Sasha chickened out. I always knew she didn't have as much guts as everyone thinks."

"What do you mean, she chickened out?" Whitney asked, frowning at the possibility her sources might have given her bad information.

"She cried like a baby and said she wanted to wait," Coco said. "They broke up over it, from what I hear. It's like I always say, the words *romance* and *camping* do not belong in the same sentence."

"That doesn't sound like Sasha," Cecily observed. "Sasha doesn't cry."

"No, she just does everything but," said Coco, snickering as Johnny reappeared to set a basket of bread on their table. The other girls quickly clammed up. He must have sensed the awkward silence, but he certainly didn't try to break it. As Johnny silently walked away, Mia excused herself to go to the restroom.

"I don't see what's so bad about Sasha wanting to wait," Cecily suddenly began. "Big deal. I think it's sort of admirable. Besides, it's not really anyone's business but theirs."

"Honey," said Coco, "if you think that boy with the apron is in the kitchen right now holding out for his precious Sasha, and not downstairs in the restroom making out with the slutty new addition to our junior class, you are sorely mistaken."

Haley gasped. Could it really be true? Were Johnny and Mia getting it on in front of everyone's noses? Coco seemed to have silenced Cecily's defense of Sasha. The girls finished their brunch without speaking, though Whitney did giggle a little when Mia emerged from the bathroom fifteen minutes later, her face flushed, her hair askew. She ordered an espresso, prompting Whitney to ask for a hot fudge sundae.

"What?" she whined as Coco glared at her. "It's a sundae on Sunday. So it's okay."

"Rationalize it any way you want to," Coco warned. "It's still a thousand calories your butt doesn't need."

"Don't listen," Mia said, diving her own spoon into the bowl of ice cream when it came. "Your butt is *magnífico*."

"*Merci,* Mia," Whitney said, gloating at Coco. "Mia, did you really model in Miami all summer?"

"*Sí, sí,* of course," Mia said. "I was in magazines, commercials."

"Really?" Coco said. "Which ones? We'll look for your pictures."

"Oh, you cannot get them here," Mia said defensively. "They are special European fashion books, European commercials, very avant-garde."

Coco still seemed suspicious.

"Uh, I just love whipped cream," Whitney exclaimed. "It's like my favorite thing on the planet. It's got everything: light, sweet, creamy, fluffy . . ." A bit of cream landed on her nose. She stuck out her tongue, trying to lick it off, but couldn't quite reach it.

"Here, Whit." Cecily passed her her napkin.

"Sometimes when I'm kissing a boy, I pretend I'm eating whipped cream," Whitney said. "It makes the whole thing so much better. Because, you know, some boys' mouths don't taste all that great—"

"*Amiga*, you are crazy," Mia said.

"Okay, Whipped Cream Queen," Coco said. "Whenever you're finished making out with your hot fudge sundae, can we get the check? Spencer's picking me up for a drive." They glanced out the window just as Spencer pulled up in his brand-new sports car.

"But we never finished talking about the costumes," Whitney said. "For the play? I'm supposed to buy fabric this week." Whitney was now chasing Coco out the door.

"I'll e-mail you later," Coco said, climbing into the passenger seat.

"I should be spending more time at Bubbies," Spencer said, peering over his aviators to get a better look at the hotties spilling out of the restaurant.

"Helllo," Mia purred, looking back at Spencer seductively.

Uh-oh, Haley thought, bracing herself. Coco might toy with Mia among the girls, but around Spencer, the younger De Clerq had a no-mercy strategy.

"The car, it's Italian?" Mia asked, her mouth curving into a pout.

Spencer was about to respond when he caught himself, patted Coco on the knee and said, "Later, girls," before speeding away.

Whitney seems to be in heaven, immersed in gossip, whipped cream and costumes. But wait a second here...did Sasha and Johnny actually "do it" in Virginia, or did Sasha freak out instead? Will Whitney be known as the Whipped Cream Queen from now on, thanks to her bordering-on-fetishistic love of the fluffy stuff? And what about Mia? Did she really model in Miami, or is she exaggerating her credentials?

There is a lot more gossip where that came from. To send Haley to Whitney's house to find out more dirt, go to page 186 (RUMOR MILL). If, on the other hand, you think Haley is sick of Coco and the gossip grind, send her running to Sasha on page 200 (FREEDOM ROCK).

Sometimes you hear things you wish you hadn't. It's up to you to decide whether you'll fan the flames with more hot air.

When in doubt,
seek retail therapy.

B*rrr!* Feel that chill in the air?" Sasha said as Haley climbed into the front seat of Sasha's vintage Mustang. "Sweater weather. Time for some new clothes."

"Hello, Haley," Sasha's mother, Pascale, said from the backseat. "How do you like Sasha's new wheels?"

Haley knew "the Stallion" had been a gift from Pascale and that she should therefore be complimentary, but she really meant it when she said, "Sasha's got the coolest car in Hillsdale."

The first stop on their shopping trip to find a new fall wardrobe: Mimi's Boutique, which had just begun carrying Whitney Klein's new fashion label, WK. (All the labels had hearts around the initials.)

"It's pretty impressive that Mimi's has picked up Whitney's line," Pascale said supportively as they pulled up in front of the former fast-food chain that Mimi had converted into a groovy fashion mecca.

"Yeah," Sasha said. "Whitney's living proof that nobody's bad at *everything*."

"Sasha!" Pascale scolded, even though she too was laughing. "That's not nice."

"Maybe a little of Johnny's sarcasm is rubbing off on you," Haley said, only half joking.

"Ha," Sasha said vaguely. "Like I've seen enough of him lately for *anything* to rub off."

The trio sauntered into the store. Mimi was busy with a couple of taut, tanned middle-aged women covered in gold jewelry. Haley couldn't help but notice that Pascale put them to shame. Pascale was about their age or even older, but she seemed ageless, while they all looked beyond their years, and worse, foolish for trying so hard to cling to their youth. Pascale's figure was still long and lean. The simple, neat bob of her hair and minimal makeup only enhanced the overall appearance. Sasha, Haley was sure, would age well.

"I'll be with you in a minute," Mimi said, glancing up at them. She nodded at a rack of clothes along one wall. "Have you girls seen the new WK line? It's doing very well." The "girls" was meant to· include Pascale. Mimi assumed she was Sasha and Haley's age.

The girls headed for the WK rack while Pascale looked at cashmere sweaters. "This stuff isn't too bad," Sasha said, holding up one of Whitney's pieces, a blue silk top with a loose tie at the front. "Kind of says sassy secretary."

"What about this, Sash?" Haley pulled out a chemise made from old soccer jerseys that had been ripped apart and resewn into a sporty minidress. "It's so you: it says soccer and rocker at the same time. I bet you're what inspired Whitney to make it."

"I doubt that," Sasha said. "Whitney's idea of inspiration was always more Coco and country club than me."

"I don't know," Haley said skeptically. "This looks like I pulled it straight out of your closet."

"Oh, that is adorable." Pascale came over and held up the minidress. "Try it on, *chérie*."

"I bet Johnny would love it," Haley offered.

Haley thought Sasha paled at the second mention of Johnny, but she couldn't be sure. "I dress to please myself, not Johnny," Sasha said emphatically.

"Of course you do," Haley said, backtracking.

"French women always dress with a man in mind," Pascale said. "And I have the overstuffed lingerie drawer to prove it."

Haley laughed, but Sasha just frowned and took the minidress into the dressing room.

"Haley, I think this green skirt would look just darling on you," Pascale added. "Why don't you try it on?"

"Thanks." Haley took the skirt, grateful for any input from Sasha's überfashionable mom. There were only two dressing rooms, and one of them was occupied by a member of the middle-aged lady tribe, so Haley poked her head through the curtain of Sasha's booth and said, "Can I come in?"

"Sure." Sasha pulled the curtain aside, now wearing the minidress.

"That looks awesome," Haley said, even though there was very little that didn't look amazing on the supertall, naturally thin Sasha.

"I don't know," Sasha said. "Maybe soccer jerseys are best left on the field."

Haley stepped into the dressing room and tried on her find, while Sasha changed out of the WK ensemble. The skirt, true to Pascale's fabulous eye, fit Haley perfectly. But somehow she couldn't enjoy the moment. Not with Sasha so obviously preoccupied.

Haley decided to take advantage of the dressing-room privacy to find out what was on Sasha's mind. "So fess up, what's up with Johnny?" she asked. "You two having problems again?" A certain story was currently making the rounds, about Sasha and Johnny's summer camping trip to Virginia.

"It's just junior year," Sasha said unconvincingly. "You know how it is. It's messing with all of our brains."

Somehow Haley wouldn't have thought junior-year craziness would affect supercool Johnny. She wasn't even sure he was planning on applying to colleges next year. But before she had a chance to probe further, Sasha changed the subject. "On to more important matters. I heard some gossip about you, Haley. Someone has a crush on you. . . ."

Haley couldn't believe her ears. Someone had a crush? *On her?* "I don't believe you. Who?" Haley asked tentatively.

"Alex Martin," Sasha blurted out. "He's a senior, but I heard he has a severe case of Haley-itis."

"Alex Martin? Really?" Haley blushed, totally flattered. Alex was cocaptain of the debate team and brilliant. He was also very cute, in a clean-cut prepster sort of way. "Who told you?"

Sasha shrugged. "It came through the grapevine, a very reliable grapevine. So, do you like him or what?"

"Um, I don't know," Haley said. "I mean, I guess I'd have to think about it." She was excited by the idea that Alex liked her, but disturbed to know people were talking about her behind her back and finding out things about her before she did. Who was on this "grapevine," anyway? And what else were people saying about her?

Haley was smart enough to know that rumors

could fly around Hillsdale High like lightning in an electrical storm. The talk was usually bad. And often not true.

"Have you heard anything else about me lately?" she asked Sasha.

"What—that's not enough for you?" Sasha teased. Haley blushed. She hoped if something bad did ever circulate about her, Sasha would tell her.

"Haley, how is the skirt?" Pascale called from outside the dressing room.

"Perfect," Haley said. "I'm going to get it." She scooped up the green garment and exited the dressing room, heading toward the register. She still had a feeling that Sasha was hiding something, but Johnny's name didn't come up again for the rest of the afternoon. Haley wondered if maybe she hadn't heard the last of Johnny Lane for a while.

● ● ●

Looks as though Sasha just pulled a fast one on Haley. What is going on with her and Johnny? Are all the rumors true? Did they really go all the way in Virginia, or did Sasha chicken out? And why won't Sasha talk about it?

Haley may soon have boy troubles herself.

What's with the report about Alex Martin's crush? Does he really have a thing for Haley—or was Sasha just making that up to get out of the hot seat? And what will Reese Highland have to say about that?

If you want Haley to stick with Sasha and make sure everything's okay in the rocker-relationship realm, go to page 200 (FREEDOM ROCK). If you think Haley should tend to her own relationships instead, send her off on a library date with Reese on page 196 (SOLVING FOR EX). Finally, if you think Haley is getting addicted to gossip and needs another quick fix, go to page 186 (RUMOR MILL).

Sometimes in life, you don't end up with what you were originally looking for. Just like sometimes you go out shopping for sweaters and come home with a skirt instead. But who's Haley's skirt? Alex or Reese?

SET DESIGN

Behind the curtain, there exists a multitude of worlds.

"The forest has to be magical," Irene said. "It has to look real, yet better than real, know what I mean?"

"Totally," Garrett "the Troll" Noll said as he jumped over three buckets of paint on his skateboard. "Like when you're a little too high on weed and everything looks kind of shimmery?"

"Um . . . sort of," Irene said. "Good try, Troll."

Haley took a couple of large white shirts from the pile of rags Devon had brought from Jack's, the vintage store where he worked after school, and fashioned them into a smock. She and the others had gathered together to help Irene paint the sets for *A Midsummer Night's Dream,* a new production the high school drama department was putting on. Irene had spread out on tarps in the Hillsdale parking lot to give them enough space to work. She brought cardboard, paper, wood, paint and all the tools necessary to create a really rad forest. Garrett and his friend Chopper zipped around on their skateboards, offering comments if not actual assistance. But all in all, they were making good progress.

"Isn't Shaun going to help?" Haley asked Irene.

"He's coming later," Irene said. "After he gets done with his postrehearsal rehearsal. Coco kept him late again."

"I bet she's driving him crazy," Haley said. "She's trying to make everyone conform to her 'vision,' even though she can't seem to say what that vision is, exactly. Why did anyone think it would be a good idea to make her assistant director?"

"Um, that would be because good old Maurice De Clerq is paying for the production," Devon interjected.

"Coco knows as much about the theater as, oh, I don't know, Chopper," Haley said snarkily, just as Chopper skidded to a showy stop on his board.

"Hey. I resent that," Chopper said.

"What's the last play you saw?" Devon said to him. Devon lifted the camera he almost always wore around his neck and snapped a shot of Chopper's in-dignant but utterly confused face.

"You really want to know?" Chopper said sud-denly. "It was *The Lion King,* school field trip, sixth grade. Remember that, Troll? With the puppets? That show was wicked sweet."

"I'd like to see it again in a different state of mind, if you get my drift," Garrett replied. He dashed across ten parking spots, looking like a black flash in his all-black clothes and black skullcap.

"That's not a bad comparison, actually," Irene said. "*The Lion King* has a mythical quality that would work well with this play, too."

Chopper lifted his board over his head and victory-danced around Devon. "See, McKnight? You thought I was going to say something dumb but I showed you up good, man."

Devon shot Chopper's victory dance, and soon Chopper had forgotten about showing him up and was just posing for the camera. That afternoon, Devon was wearing an apron to protect his brown pullover and blue cords from paint. Haley thought she'd never seen an apron look so good. People seemed to perform for Devon without even realizing it. Haley enjoyed taking photos too, but the trick was to get the subjects to forget the camera was there, and Devon was somehow able to do that.

Irene pulled out her sketchbook and all her draw-ings of forests. "This is the basic layout," she said, pointing her pencil to a particular scene: summer trees in full bloom, a low yellow moon, flowers and toadstools to serve as fairy furniture and tree branches with bowers as cozy as hammocks for the lovers. Haley was amazed at how Irene could evoke a whole world with just a few quick strokes.

"Use as many different shades of green as you can on the trees," Irene said. "Lighter tones on the places where the moonlight shines, and darker, richer greens for the deep, spooky underbrush. And plenty of gold and silver, too. The forest should look like a palace."

"Those are some wicked fine drawings," Garrett said, peering over Irene's shoulder. "That place would make a perfect hideout, if you were ever, say, running from the cops."

Everyone looked up at Garrett, wondering if he was having any trouble with the law. "Hey, wait a minute," the Troll said, realizing all eyes were on him. "I said 'If.' If a person, any person, found himself running from the cops. Not me personally."

"It *is* an incredible drawing," Haley agreed.

"You should have seen how she just whipped it off like it was nothing," Devon said, snapping a shot of the sketch.

"Big deal," Irene said. "This and a bucket of paint will get you a gig making sets for a school play. Oh wait—I *am* making sets for a school play. How friggin' glamorous."

"No, really," Haley said. "Do your parents understand what a gift you have?"

"My parents think I make a mean egg roll," Irene said sarcastically.

What a shame, Haley thought. Irene was so incredibly talented, and her parents' dream for her was that she'd take over the family business. Working at the Golden Dynasty was so limiting, and not what Irene was interested in at all. But sometimes Haley got the feeling Irene didn't have the will to defy her parents—as if she was afraid to disappoint them.

"Heee-hawww. Heeee-hawww." Shaun burst out of the building, still wearing his donkey-head costume. " 'What sayst thou, bully Bottom?' "

Irene sighed. "Oh, Shaunster, off with the head. You can't paint with that thing on."

" 'I will undertake it. What beard were I best to play it in? I will discharge it in either your straw-colour beard, your orange-tawny beard, your purple-in-grain beard, or your French-crown-colour beard, your perfect yellow.' " Shaun recited his lines in an accent that was half English, half Spicoli in *Fast Times at Ridgemont High.*

"What was that, man?" Chopper asked. "You talking backwards again?"

"Krej uoy, ton m'I, on," Shaun said.

"Whatever, man," Chopper said. "I can't hack that."

"Talk normal or shut up," Garrett added.

"It's Shakespeare, you dorks," Devon said. "Or it was until Shaun got ahold of it."

"That's what I'm talking about," Chopper said.

Shaun stuck his papier-mâché donkey's head right in Irene's face and hee-hawed at her again. Then he stood on his hands and did a few donkey kicks for good measure.

"This donkey thing is getting old," Irene said. "Fast."

"So old," Haley agreed. "Ancient."

"Dudes, *hee*—what about the—*haw*—Method?" Shaun said. "I've got to stay in character until the play's done. I shouldn't even be saying this in normal talk. I should be speaking Shakespeare-Donkeytalk twenty-four/seven."

"Go ahead and do that," Devon said. "If you want to spend the next few weeks talking to yourself."

"Really, Shaun," Irene said. "It's one thing to practice your lines. But I am not going out in public with you wearing that donkey head. It's bad enough at school."

"Rini, you're an artist," Shaun said. "You get me. I'm doing this for my art."

He tried to nuzzle her, but she shoved him away. "Ew, that thing is starting to smell."

● ● ●

Shaun sure has a tendency to go off the deep end with his obsessions. Usually, Irene is pretty understanding, but this donkey act seems to be grating on even her nerves. If he's going to be wearing that donkey head everywhere and braying all the time, how will Irene be able to concentrate on the elaborate forest paintings she's creating? Then again, if you're going to go onstage in front of the whole school, you've got to go all out. And no one knows how to let it all hang out better than Shaun.

To keep Haley in the theater groove, wander deeper into the wacky forest on page 207 (OFF-OFF-OFF-BROADWAY). If you think Haley needs a break from the weirdness, send her to check up on Annie and Dave on page 180 (SCATTERBRAINED). To thine own self be true. But which of Haley's selves deserves to be heard?

SCATTERBRAINED

College mania is a disease— and one that's highly contagious.

"No, Haley, you don't get it." Beads of sweat popped up on Dave Metzger's forehead, even though the window was wide open and his room was freezing. ("For better brain stimulation," Annie Armstrong had said when she opened it, and let in the frigid breeze.) Haley put her sweater back on and huddled on the rug beside them.

"It's not that simple," Dave was saying. "You can't write a one-size-fits-all essay for all the colleges. You have to tailor each one to what the school is looking for. Each institution has its own personality. It wants students who'll fit in. Look at the chart." He stabbed his finger on the huge poster laid out in front of them on the floor. It was a flow chart Dave and Annie had made of all the top colleges: their requirements, locations, stats on the student body, pros and cons about each.

"See, Brown and Berkeley like free thinkers, but Stanford usually takes a more conventional student," Annie said, running her finger along the lines connecting the schools. "For Harvard, you have to be more rigorous. You have to 'show your work,' in a way."

Haley nodded, even though she had no idea what they were talking about. Annie and Dave were so stressed over colleges, Haley was beginning to worry they were losing their minds. Dave's hives had returned, full force. The slightest disagreement brought unsightly rashes to his arms, neck and face. Annie had even whispered to Haley that Dave now had serious backne—a sure sign of overstress and an overshare, to say the least. Meanwhile, Annie herself was so frantic about colleges, the subject had invaded her every conversation. Ask about ice cream, and you ended up talking about MIT. She analyzed her every action in terms of whether or not a particular college would approve. "Would a University of Chicago student eat this apple?" she'd say, holding up a piece of fruit. "Or is that too New England for them? Maybe I should have some deep-dish pizza instead. That would put me in the right frame of mind."

Their stress was contagious, and it was getting to be too much for Haley. But, perversely, the more she heard them prattle on about Princeton versus Yale and whether Dartmouth was too frat-boy for them, the more interested Haley became. She'd always been a good student, and she'd always dreamed of going to a prestigious college, too. But now that it was time to apply, Haley realized how much work was involved, and how insanely competitive it was. Dave's sweaty, zit-covered face was proof enough of that.

"I keep switching my number one between Yale and MIT," Dave said, holding up a list of colleges he was applying to, with twenty-five slots and multiple cross-outs and write-overs. "But then I think, shouldn't it be Harvard? I mean, Harvard's number one in the eyes of most of the world. Who am I to argue with that?"

"You put Harvard number three because you went to computer camp instead of studying philosophy with a tutor last summer, remember?" Annie said. "Didn't you read somewhere that Harvard prefers students with a philosophical turn of mind? Or did I dream that?"

"True," Dave said. "And the MIT rep I talked to last year seemed much more impressed with my podcast than any of the Ivies."

"I just hope my transcript isn't too nerdy," Annie

said. "I mean, I love the debate team, but is it too cliché-smart-kid? Haley?"

"If you love it you should do it," Haley said. "That's what I say."

"That kind of thinking will get you nowhere," Dave said. "What are your top five, Haley?"

"I haven't ranked them yet, but I'm thinking Brown, Yale, Columbia, maybe Wesleyan—"

"Don't count on Wesleyan as a backup," Annie warned. "Those days are long gone."

"Or Oberlin either," Dave said.

"I wasn't counting it as a backup," Haley said.

"You should definitely apply to Columbia," Annie said. "I mean, your dad teaches there, right? That can't hurt."

"Unless the administration doesn't like him for some reason." Dave scratched his neck frantically while he spoke.

"Why wouldn't the administration like my dad?" Haley said.

"Never know," Dave said.

Hanging with Annie and Dave certainly wasn't much fun these days, but they'd done so much research on every college that Haley thought it had to be helping her get her thoughts together. She now understood what she needed to do: prepare as much as possible for every debate, study more for all her classes and do an extra SAT prep practice test every night before bed. Among a million other things.

"Brown has a good media department," Dave said. "If I want to impress their semiotics profs, I've got to take 'Inside Hillsdale' live as a videocast. By next week."

"You're taking the podcast to video?" Haley asked. Dave was famous for "Inside Hillsdale," his weekly podcast on topics of interest to Hillsdale High students, including live interviews. But it was one thing to do an audio-only radio-style program every week. It was a lot more complicated to go video—and, in Dave's case, maybe not advisable until his little sweating problem and breakouts had cleared up. He had, as they say, a face for radio.

"Slow down, you guys," Haley said. "How is it humanly possible to do all this work? Don't you think we might be taking on too much at once? Anyone? Dave?"

"Haley, it's not as if I or Dave is going to get recruited for sports," Annie said, and truer words were never spoken. "There are thousands of smart kids out there with perfect GPAs and SAT scores, trying to get the attention of these admissions officers. We've got to do everything we can. And we've got to start now."

"You never know which one detail will make them remember you," Dave added.

"I guess," Haley said. She was beginning to wonder if she maybe didn't prefer the old post-Spain-Spring-break Annie and Dave, the slackers who had thrown grades, rules and the precious Ivies to the wind.

● ● ●

Leave it to Dave and Annie to organize and obsess over their college applications as if preparing for World War III. Still, Haley wants to get into the school of her dreams, whatever that turns out to be, so at least in some small way, she can understand Dave and Annie's anxiety. But does Haley have any idea what college she wants to go to? Or is she waiting to find out how she does on the SATs before she deals with any of that?

If you think Haley should be there when Dave launches the VIDEOCAST, turn to page 214. If you think Haley should remember to stay well rounded—and sane—go to PRINCIPAL CRUM'S LITANY on page 226.

The best colleges want the best minds. Losing your mind is not the best strategy for getting in.

What goes around comes around . . . and around, and around . . .

"Manor Estates?" Coco sniffed as they rode through the front gates of a brand-new luxury housing development, where not even the guesthouses were smaller than two thousand square feet. "*Très* nouveau. You know they build these shacks with particle board and wood glue, right?"

Haley sat in the front seat of the hybrid SUV, her mom driving, Coco in the backseat, which did not exactly make the teen queen happy. They were on their way to hang with Whitney at the new house of the ex–Mrs. Klein, who was now living with Sasha Lewis's father, Jonathan Lewis. It was a long, complicated and slightly sordid tale, but in the end, the coupling seemed to be working out nicely.

"I think it's great that Linda Klein has pulled her life together," Joan Miller said, frowning at Coco in the rearview mirror. "After what that devil of a husband did to her."

The previous year, Whitney's dad, New Jersey's breath-spray king, had left his first wife for a much younger waitress at the country club—an unsavory tart named Trish. Devastated and temporarily locked out of all her bank accounts, Linda Klein had taken Whitney to live in a depressing apartment in the Floods. It was around that time when Linda reconnected with Jonathan, a recovering gambler and alcoholic, who was also in the process of hitting rock bottom. They became friends, then fell in love, and now seemed to be in the midst of a sharp lifestyle upgrade—with a little help, of course, from Linda's ample divorce settlement and her steady income from her newly instated broker's license. Linda was actually a partner in the Manor Estates subdivision.

Haley was surprised to hear how much her mom knew about the personal lives of her friends' parents. Were rumors running so rampant in Hillsdale that even love-thy-neighbor Joan Miller was in the loop? "Since when are you so up on the gossip, Mom?"

"Oh, you know," Joan said. "If you spend

enough time with Blythe Armstrong, you just start to absorb this stuff through osmosis." Joan worked at the same environmental law firm as Annie Armstrong's mother, and though they were die-hard do-gooders, they evidently weren't above a little friendly chatter.

Personally, Haley was glad for Whitney. Living in the Floods had been hard for someone as status-conscious as she was.

"Ew," shrieked Coco, "who picked out these plants? The colors are so ghetto." The development was so new half the lawns hadn't been sodded yet, and the other half had explosions of overly bright mums hastily stuck into the ground.

Joan pulled into the circular drive in front of Whitney's new house, a faux-Tudor-style manor that seemed to be as big as or bigger than the original Klein McMansion.

"Well, it's certainly not my taste," Joan admitted. "But I have to say, it's something, all right."

"To put it mildly," Haley said. Her mother was very much against ostentatious displays of wealth.

"Your dad will pick you up in a few hours," Joan said as the girls climbed out of the SUV. "Have fun."

"Thanks, Mom," Haley said. Coco, of course, said nothing, and emphatically brushed imagined dirt and dust off her jeans after she exited the vehicle. Haley thought it was amazingly rude of her to treat Joan like a chauffeur. Actually, even a chauffeur should be thanked. *I guess it's safe to assume the old Coco is back.*

Whitney greeted them at the door, clearly house-proud. "Come on in," she said, teetering through the half-empty front hall in feathered, high-heeled mules and a dressing gown. "We still have a ways to go with the decorating, but it's already such an improvement over our last space."

"Uh, yeah," said Coco. "A cardboard box in an alley would have been an improvement over that hovel. Please tell me you burned all your old furniture and clothes? I did not come here to get bedbugs or fleas."

"Everything's new, down to the hand towels." Whitney led them upstairs to her room. "Here it is: the Whitney hospitality suite." Suite was not a bad description of Whitney's new room, which opened onto a small living area with a sofa, chairs and a coffee table, and branched off to a work area for designing clothes on the left and a bedroom and bathroom on the right.

"Wow, Whitney, it's huge," Haley said. "It's like you have your own place!"

"There's an identical suite down the hall for Sasha," Whitney said. "Though she's never used it. I can't say I blame her. I wouldn't want to hang around with Jonathan either if I didn't have to."

"How can your mother trust him in the house?" Coco asked. "Isn't she, like, worried he's going to steal a painting and head straight for the nearest roulette wheel?"

"Mom says he's totally reformed," Whitney said. "But I don't know . . . I mean, once a gambler, always a gambler, right?"

"Whit, a diet soda," Coco demanded. "I don't want to ask for it twice."

Two seconds after Whitney left the room to get snacks, Coco turned to Haley and said, "Sasha's dad is *thisclose* to popping the question to Whitney's mom, but Whitney doesn't know it yet."

"How do you know?" Haley asked.

"I hear things," Coco said. "Somebody saw Jonathan shopping for rings in Manhattan, the diamond district. What else would he be doing there? On second thought, maybe he was hocking Linda's jewelry. Poor, poor woman." Coco shook her head.

"I'm sure your first guess was right," Haley said. "I wonder how Whitney will take the news. She doesn't seem too crazy about Jonathan."

"She'll be upset, of course. She'll freak, actually. Cohabitation is one thing; matrimonial vows are quite another. But I'm more curious to know how Sasha will feel." Coco arched an eyebrow. "Can you imagine, Whitney and Sasha as stepsisters? What a pair."

Whitney and Sasha had been lifelong BFFs. Until recently, that is, when Sasha had decided she was tired of the superficial Cocobot lifestyle and threw herself into practicing soccer and guitar. Whitney, meanwhile, had kept clinging to Coco as if she were a life raft.

"Don't say anything to Whitney, or she'll have a meltdown, and I cannot deal with that today. You know how emotional she gets." Coco sifted through a pile of fashion magazines on Whitney's coffee table. "Rats, she doesn't have it."

"Have what?" Haley asked.

"Oh, some European fashion magazine that trashy Mia Delgado claims she has a story in. But I don't buy it. Sure, there's a certain . . . wanton appeal about the girl. But no way is she top-model material. I think she's making up all this modeling business—and I'm going to prove it."

Coco sat back on the couch and waited for Haley to beg for more info. At that moment, Whitney rushed back into the room. "WhudImiss, whudImiss?"

"Coco was just filling me in on her theories about Mia Delgado," Haley said, irritated that the conversation had once again shifted to the stunning Spanish mannequin. No matter where she went these days, everyone always seemed to be talking about Mia.

"Ooh, have you heard the latest?" Whitney nosed in, realizing she had a bit of news she had yet to share with the group. That was the thing about Whitney. She heard lots of juicy stuff, some of it true, some of it false. But as often as not, rumors flew out of Whitney's head before she had time to pass them on. You had to catch her at just the right moment, such as right after a visit to her hair salon, and then, without applying too much pressure, coax the volcano of rumors that was Whitney Klein to erupt.

"Do tell," Coco encouraged, without seeming too eager.

"Well, apparently, Drew Napolitano heard Mia arguing with Sebastian. About a tape."

"What sort of tape?" Coco imperceptibly leaned forward, suppressing her curiosity.

"A tape apparently made by someone Mia used to date. Someone who wasn't Sebastian Bodega. And," Whitney added, a wicked grin on her face, "it's a naked tape." She whispered those last three words, scandalized by the thought of such salacious viewing material.

"No," Haley gasped.

"Yup," said Whitney. "Mia was denying it, but Sebastian is not happy. And he said if her modeling agency ever caught wind of it, or actually saw the tape, her career would be over."

"You don't say," Coco mused.

Whitney grabbed three tortilla chips and loaded them with guac. But now it was her appetite for gossip that needed to be sated. "Have you two heard about what the football team's been up to lately? Cecily told me that Drew told her but swore her to secrecy."

"Figures," said Coco.

"But luckily, I have my own sources. It's called the booster club. Here's what I know—the varsity players are hazing the freshmen, saying if they want to be part of the team they've got to do whatever the upperclassmen say."

"Like what?" Haley asked innocently.

"I can't believe what idiots boys can be." Coco sighed. "Thank goodness my Spencer's not immature like that."

"Right," Haley said. "Spencer's real mature. He only runs an illegal gambling ring."

"It may be illegal but it's certainly not childish," Coco said. "And besides, he's given that up because of the campaign. So tell us, Whit, what exactly do the football players do?"

"Well, I heard they took one kid and blindfolded him and made him take off all his clothes and walk through town at midnight," Whitney said. "In his jockstrap. And his father happened to drive by and see him, but he must not have recognized him because he didn't stop. And when another kid said he didn't want to do it, they filled his locker with manure."

"Yuck," Haley said. "Why aren't they getting in trouble for all this?"

"Because the freshmen grunts are too afraid to squeal," Whitney said. "And the older boys took a vow of silence or something."

"I guess the vow of silence doesn't apply to girl-friends," Coco said, thinking of Cecily and Drew.

"Guess not," Haley agreed.

● ● ●

There seems to be an awful lot of gossip swirling around Hillsdale these days. It's enough to make Haley's head spin. If even her highly principled mother is capable of getting caught up in the rumor mill, who is Haley to resist spreading the word?

Sasha's dad is about to propose to Whitney's mom, and neither girl knows anything about it? That's big—and maybe Sasha and Whitney have a right to know. It's their lives too, after all. Of course, if that rumor isn't true, it could cause a lot of damage for nothing.

And what about the sports hazing—shouldn't people know about that? Or should Haley leave it up to the victims themselves to turn in their tormentors?

The juiciest rumor by far is Mia's scandalous love tape. This one's the most tempting to spread, because of Mia's man-eater status. With her around, the other girls hardly stand a chance. Shouldn't all those admiring boys know what kind of girl they're drooling over? Or would that just make them drool even more?

If you think Haley should be TALKING TRASH, spreading the rumors she's just heard around the school, go to page 219. If you think she should not get involved in any of this, have her take the HIGH ROAD on page

223. And if you're not sure what Haley should do, and want to find out more before making a decision, send her to hear PRINCIPAL CRUM'S LITANY on page 226.

Some people love to hear gossip from their friends, but not so much when the gossip is about them.

Some people never learn—
not even in the library.

"**S**o, what are you doing your history research paper on?" Reese asked as Haley waltzed into the library for their "date." The very idea of having a date at the library seemed suspect to Haley, but she wanted to give Reese the benefit of the doubt. Maybe he had some kind of bookish surprise cooked up for her. The fact that the first words out of his mouth were about their AP history paper didn't exactly seem like a good sign.

"I was thinking of comparing the presidencies of

John Adams and John Quincy Adams," Haley said as she settled at a study table next to him. "You?"

"Teapot Dome Scandal," Reese said. "We're not getting to it until the end of the semester but that means I'll have a head start."

"Smart move," Haley said.

Reese got up and headed into the aisles of books in search of twentieth-century history. Haley started to follow him, wondering if he might try to steal a kiss among the stacks, but he pointed her to the next row and said, "I think the eighteenth century is in that stack over there."

"Oh," she said. "Thanks." *This has to be the most prudish, boring date in the history of romance,* she thought as she halfheartedly scanned the rows of presidential biographies. She waited for Reese to find his book and then find her, but he didn't reappear. *This can't be all there is,* she thought, and turned the corner to find him engrossed in a pile of books.

"What are you doing Friday night?" she asked, hoping to salvage this sad date by setting up another. "Want to get together, and, I don't know, go to a movie? Make out in my basement?"

"Actually, we're having our freshman initiation Friday night," Reese said, barely lifting his head from the book he was reading. He was a star of the soccer team, and the upperclassman players had a tradition of initiating the freshman kickers at a special party every fall. Haley wasn't sure exactly what went on at those events—they were shrouded in mystery and rumor. But she and her cocaptain, Sasha, had always thought the girls' soccer team should have an initiation party too. After all, if it was good enough for the boys, it was good enough for them too.

"That's cool," Haley said. "Sasha and I thought it might be fun to have a coed soccer initiation this year. Maybe we could team up with you guys on Friday night? What do you think?"

"Sure, whatever you want," Reese said, but Haley wasn't sure he'd heard her suggestion. And even if he had heard her, it wasn't clear from his lackluster response how he really felt about the idea. Were the girls welcome, or did he think they were horning in on the boys' fun?

With a sigh Haley sank to the carpeted library floor and watched, bored out of her mind, while Reese studied. *This sucks,* she thought. Just then, Devon McKnight passed by her carrying a bound copy of *A Midsummer Night's Dream,* the drama club's next play. She found herself watching Devon as he strutted over to the counter and checked out the book. *What would it be like to spend time alone with him?* Haley wondered. *Would he be as boring as Reese, or could something actually heat up?*

●　●　●

This library date with Reese is obviously going nowhere. What was he thinking? And what was *Haley* thinking when she agreed to it in the first place? Reese is so caught up in his studies this year, he is barely listening to a word Haley says.

How much of this is Haley willing to tolerate at this stage in their relationship? It could be just a phase, and if she waits it out, the old, charming Reese may return to her. Or maybe not. Meanwhile, arty photographer Devon is looking pretty hot right about now, and at least he's doing something more interesting than burying his head in a book. Oh wait, maybe not.

If you think Haley should ditch Reese and find out what Devon's up to, go to page 235 (RUN LINES WITH DEVON). If you think she's serious about having a coed initiation, no matter what Reese says, send her to the INITIATION on page 231. Finally, you can hear the latest Hillsdale High gossip on page 226 (PRINCIPAL CRUM'S LITANY).

Every relationship hits a snag once in a while. But is this a minor bump in the road or a serious dead end? It's up to you to steer Haley in the right direction.

Rock shows tend to bring out the blockheads.

"I can't wait to see these bands," Haley said, growing more and more excited. She was sitting in the back-seat of Sasha's Mustang, with Johnny Lane riding shotgun as Sasha steered the car down the Garden State Parkway to the George Washington Bridge. The three of them were headed to the College Music Festival in Manhattan—a hundred bands in three days, with headliners packing into dozens of venues. Sasha's mom had bought them tickets for day two, which had a stellar lineup. Haley was actually surprised to find Johnny in the car when Sasha arrived to pick her up. The couple hadn't exactly been spending loads of time together of late. But then, Haley knew Johnny would never pass up a music festival with this caliber of talent. And Sasha would never be able to go to one without him.

"Wait 'til you see this first performance," Sasha said, turning to Johnny and grinning. "Twenty-five musicians onstage, dancers, fire-eaters, fiddlers, a chorus—"

"It's Thai dinner theater meets the Grand Ol' Opry," Haley offered.

"That's cool for some bands," said Johnny. "But I don't get it. It's not the Hedon. Lately I've been thinking we should be paring things down, not cluttering them up."

Johnny was the lead guitarist for one of the best local bands in Hillsdale. Their sound was raw seventies garage rock, and there was most definitely no room for fiddlers or fire-eaters on their stage. Even so, Haley thought Johnny should be a little more generous. Sasha had, after all, gotten them the tickets.

A few months back, Sasha had had a stint with the Hedon. But she had quit to go solo as a singer-songwriter over the summer. Haley believed that decision had probably saved Sasha and Johnny's relationship, or what was left of it anyway. Through Sasha, Haley had seen firsthand the tension and infighting that could spring up between bandmates. "Now I know why the Beatles broke up," Sasha had put it at the time.

Haley stared out the window as the Mustang flew over the GW Bridge. Across the Hudson, the New York City skyline reflected the golden sunlight of a crisp fall Saturday. Haley felt a surge of excitement every time she crossed the river into the city. She'd felt the same way in California, driving from her home in Marin County into San Francisco. But NYC had an energy even San Fran couldn't match—anything could happen here. You never knew whom you'd meet.

"Is there anything you do really want to see?" Sasha asked Johnny, anxiously awaiting his response.

"Well, it'll be great to see some new blood," Johnny said. "We all got so hyped up over that Battle of the Bands competition last spring, we lost our sense of mission. We need to get back to our roots. Forget Rubber Dynamite. Our real competition is in here. We should be modeling ourselves on the friggin' Stones, man."

Sasha laughed. "Nothing like keeping your expectations low."

They drove down the FDR Drive and, just as quickly as they'd entered Manhattan, they exited it, heading over the Williamsburg Bridge into Brooklyn. The first festival event was to be held at a warehouse-sized club called the Lo-Fi. A crowd of hipsters jammed the entrance, hoping to snag tickets for the sold-out show. Sasha, Haley and Johnny pushed through the crowd, waved their tickets at the bouncer and went inside. Haley felt like she fit right in, wearing an old Sonic Youth T-shirt she had borrowed from Sasha with skinny jeans tucked into slouchy eighties boots. Those had been picked up for a song at Jack's Vintage. Sasha looked equally cool in plaid leggings, motorcycle boots and a black knit minidress under a leather jacket. Johnny, meanwhile, wore his standard uniform: black jeans, plain black tee, tinted glasses and his signature slouch.

One of the opening bands was already onstage, pounding out a funk-metal riff. "I'm going to get a bottle of water," Haley shouted to Sasha over the music. "Need anything?"

"I'm good," Sasha said. Johnny gave a nod, meaning if he needed anything, he'd handle it himself.

Haley headed for the bar, just as she was ordering her sparkling water, someone tugged on her sleeve. "I always say New York is just a small town in disguise." Haley turned around and was shocked to see Alex Martin, of all people, grinning at her. He stood out among the rocker crowd in his neat button-down shirt, and khakis, but he didn't seem to be self-conscious about it—maybe because he had two VIP press passes dangling from his neck.

"What are you doing here?" she asked.

"Covering the show for the College Music Festival Web site," Alex said. "They don't pay but I do get to hang in the VIP area—best seats in the house."

"It's standing room only," Haley reminded him, looking up at the balcony and over at the roped-off pit near the stage.

"Right," Alex said, pursing his lips.

"How did you get the gig, anyway? You're not in college," Haley asked.

"A minor technicality," Alex said. "Besides, they like to groom their writers young."

Haley nodded. Alex was certainly different from most of the guys she knew in Hillsdale—and there seemed to be a lot she didn't know about him yet.

As the opening band finished their set and cleared the stage, a trio of roadies prepped the equipment for the next act.

"Come on," Alex suddenly blurted out. "Let's go get a good spot near the stage." He took off one of his press passes and hung it around Haley's neck.

"Thanks," Haley said, taking his hand as they wove their way through the crowd, flashing their passes at a guard standing by a roped-off area. Haley waved to Sasha to let her know she was okay. Sasha smiled when she saw Alex and gave Haley a big thumbs-up. They reached the front of the stage—just in time for the first song. The band started playing, and Haley could see everything. She'd never been so close to a famous act before. She danced and sang along with her favorite songs, with Alex right beside her.

"That was amazing," she said to Alex when the set was over. "I think I actually have some of the band's sweat on me."

"Let's hope that's not all yours," Alex said, pointing to Haley's damp T-shirt. They wandered out of the VIP area and back through the club, where they found Sasha and Johnny leaning against the bar, drinking energy drinks.

"Hey! How was the view from the expensive seats?" Sasha asked.

Haley showed off her VIP press pass. "Let's just say I had a moment with one of the fiddle players. Do you guys know Alex?"

Johnny gave him a nod. "Hey, man. Way to score passes."

"That's Johnny, I'm Sasha," Sasha said, making the unnecessary introductions.

"Yeah, I know who you guys are. Listen, I'd better go scribble some notes on the show before I forget all the details," Alex said. "See you later, Haley?"

"Sure, Alex," Haley said, "and thanks."

Alex blushed a little as he waved goodbye.

"Highland who?" Johnny said under his breath.

"Ready to roll, Hale?" Sasha asked, frowning at Johnny. They all headed outside to the car to drive to the next act.

"It's too bad we can't come into the city like this

every weekend," Haley observed. Somehow, she didn't think her parents would be down with that. It'd been hard enough getting them to let her out of the house for this.

"Ahem, we've got soccer team initiation next weekend, remember, Cap?" Sasha said, turning to Haley. "Those frosh aren't going to initiate themselves."

Johnny scoffed.

"Right," Haley said, remembering their commitment. She couldn't help but wonder if maybe there wasn't a more productive way to spend her time, though. Like, say, getting better acquainted with a certain senior?

● ● ●

What a coincidence running into Alex like that. Or was it a fated encounter? Who knew the master debater and math champ was also a published—albeit unpaid—rock journalist? What else is the superstar senior capable of?

Ready or not, frosh, here come the soccer captains. If you want to skip the school week and go straight to the INITIATION, turn to page 231. If you think Haley's having second thoughts and would rather figure out a way to bump into Alex instead, go to PRINCIPAL CRUM'S LITANY on page 226.

All it takes to start a rumor is one little sighting, say of a junior girl and a senior guy dancing in front of a stage in Williamsburg. So what will Reese Highland have to say when he hears this one?

OFF-OFF-OFF-BROADWAY

Those who can, do. Those who can't do, teach. Those who can't teach, teach gym. Or sometimes drama.

"I didn't expect the theater to be so tiny," Haley said. She, Shaun, Devon and Irene had made a trip into the city to see their tutor, Xavier, make his Off-Off-Off-Broadway debut in a new play called *The Soul Farmer*. Shaun was especially excited to see his cousin at work.

"The Hillsdale High auditorium puts this place to shame," Irene said.

"No, it's cool," Shaun said. "It's gritty. Real. *Heehaw.*"

"It's real, all right," Irene said. "Like this delusion that you're an ass. Oh wait, it's not a delusion, it's true."

"I'm not crazy about the title," Devon said. "*The Soul Farmer?* It's a bit too Elmer Gantry for me."

"It is a little creepy," Haley agreed. "But we've got to watch for Xavier's sake. He's certainly suffered through enough of our performances at this point."

"I'm this close to naming him my guru," Shaun said. "Haw. Haw." Thankfully, Irene had managed to convince him to leave his donkey head at home, saying it wouldn't fit in Devon's little car. But he was still bringing his donkey persona along wherever he went.

They took their seats. Haley's was sunken and tilted slightly to the right. She would have moved over one but the next seat had gum on it.

Xavier just finished drama school, she told herself. *Everyone has to start somewhere.*

After a few minutes, the lights went down and the curtain went up. The setting was a shack in a cornfield. Xavier appeared wearing overalls and a straw hat, no shirt, a piece of straw between his teeth and a pitchfork in his hand. For some reason he had bright red makeup all over his face and hands.

"That's one bad farmer tan," Irene whispered to Haley, who giggled.

"Shhh!" said Shaun.

"Ha-ha-ha-ha!" Xavier shouted. "NO ONE ith thafe from me! Even on thith PEATHEFUL farm, where the THINTH and tempTATIONTH of the thity are out of reach. I thtill wreak my HAVOC. Ha-ha!"

"What the . . . ?" Devon whispered.

Xavier was doing that thing he always did, talking WITH GREAT EMPHASIS on certain WORDS. Haley had thought he'd at least try to get into character, whatever this particular character was. But he just seemed to be acting . . . Xavier. Or maybe this was part of the character, in his eyes? Whatever the METHOD, this just didn't seem right.

An actress entered stage left, in blond pigtails and a Dorothy-in-*The Wizard of Oz* pinafore.

"Well, howdy, stranger," she said. "Ain't you a sight for sore eyes. We don't get many visitors round these parts." She batted her eyelashes at Xavier. Haley started to laugh, thinking this was supposed to be funny, but she stifled it when no one else in the audience was laughing.

"I can thee WHY," Xavier said stiffly. "ALLOW me to INTRODUTHE mythelf. My NAME ith Bill. Bill Z. Bub."

"As in Beelzebub?" Devon whispered. "The devil?"

Haley shrugged. "I guess."

"Shh!" Shaun said again. "You guys!" But he looked worried.

There were a lot of shenanigans onstage involving Xavier's character, Bill Z. Bub, causing trouble between a farmer, his two teenaged children and the widow lady next door. Haley found it hard to follow. Finally she gave up. The play was ridiculous, and none of the actors was particularly good, but Xavier was terrible. She kept thinking he was up to something, some technique that would pay off at the end. Then, for the final scene, he walked onto the stage with his skinny body covered in red paint and nothing else.

"Oh my god," Irene gasped.

"I don't believe this," Shaun muttered.

Haley struggled not to laugh. It was nearly impossible. Xavier recited his final monologue, something about evil being banal, while Haley pinched her arm to keep herself from bursting into hysterics.

At last the curtain fell. The audience applauded, and Haley could let it out.

"So . . . do we have to go backstage and say hi?" Irene said. "Or can we just get out of here and act like that train wreck never happened?"

"I want to go straight home and take a long hot shower to wash away the memory of that red devil forever," Devon said.

"What do you think, Shaun?" Haley asked. "Will Xavier be hurt if we don't go backstage?"

Shaun was staring at the stage in shock.

"Shaun?" Irene snapped her fingers in front of his face. "Sweetie? Hee-haw?"

"He sucked," Shaun said slowly. "I can't believe how bad he just sucked."

"Yeah, it was pretty heinous," Devon said. "Next tutoring session, I think I'll use the old 'It was interesting' line. Never fails."

"But I believed in him," Shaun said. "I took his acting advice. I listened to his criticisms. I was going to make him my acting guru. I can't believe how close I came to following a phony."

"He's not a phony," Haley reassured him. "He believes all that stuff he was telling us. He's just not particularly talented at acting. I mean, the guy was born with a lisp."

"Those who can't do, teach," Devon offered.

"Come on, let's get out of here," Haley said, patting Shaun on the back. He was uncharacteristically quiet on the ride home. He didn't even utter a single *hee-haw*.

"Don't take it so hard, Shaun," Irene said. "Devon's right. Lots of amazing instructors can't do whatever it is they're teaching. Look at Mr. Von." Rick Von was their eccentric art teacher, and a favorite among students. "Remember that abstract painting of his he showed us? The one that was all black with the one little orange dot on it? Remember how shocked we all were—like, 'That's your painting? That's the best you can do?' I thought his art was going to be so much more interesting and alive than that. Because when he's teaching, it's really magic. But just because he sucked at painting, it didn't make me want to throw out my work."

Shaun remained silent.

Haley felt it was time to change the subject. "Hey, did you guys hear the latest about Mr. Von's potential future stepson, Dave Metzger?" Dave's uptight mom was currently dating Mr. Von; they made a very odd couple indeed. "Supposedly he's turning 'Inside Hillsdale' into a live videocast."

"Wow. Risky move," Devon said. "Do you think his huge and loyal following among the teenybopper set will continue once they realize that's who they've been listening to all these months?"

"Doubtful," said Haley.

"Oh, Dave will find a way to screw up," Irene said. "For sure."

● ● ●

Poor Shaun. He takes his enthusiasms so seriously. What will he do now? Is he going to give up Method acting? Irene would be relieved, but how would that affect Shaun's performance in the play? Knowing Shaun, Xavier's humiliation could drive him to take the Method mania even farther. Logic isn't exactly Shaun's strong suit.

At least Devon's kept his head. Tutoring and

rehearsing for the play have brought him and Haley closer than ever. If you think she should take advantage of their cozy closeness and spend more time alone with him, send her to page 235 (RUN LINES WITH DEVON).

If you think Haley needs a break from this scene and ought to satisfy her curiosity about Dave's new videocast, go to page 214 (VIDEOCAST). Or if you think it's time Haley found out what the rest of the school is up to, go to page 226 (PRINCIPAL CRUM'S LITANY).

Finding the right balance in life is not easy, especially if you feel pulled in different directions.

Before you let the public into your bedroom, it's a good idea to clean up.

Haley was headed to Dave's house with Annie to help out with his first-ever videocast of "Inside Hillsdale." Dave was streaming live directly from his bedroom, using his cluttered desk as a backdrop and his halogen desk lamp as a spotlight, aimed at his sweaty, pimply face.

"Does he need that light?" Haley asked as Annie bustled around trying to make him look presentable.

"Without it, viewers won't be able to see his face," Annie said.

"Exactly," Haley said. "He's really broken out. Hives on top of zits—that's pretty gruesome."

"I'll put more pancake on him," Annie said, reaching for the flesh-toned makeup. "You'd look gruesome too if you had been studying eighteen hours a day and had insomnia for three weeks straight."

"Must get into Harvard," Dave said, rocking back and forth. "Or MIT. If I don't get into one of those two, I'll take my vows and become a monk."

"What? That's crazy. We won't even get to apply to schools for another year yet," Haley said. She glanced at Annie, who nodded knowingly. "You're pushing yourself too hard, Dave."

"No such thing," Dave said. "No such thing." He wiped his damp brow, removing a lot of the makeup in the process. He stared at his handkerchief, dazed. "Oh, look, my skin's coming off."

"That's just makeup," Annie said. "Your skin is fine. Or, well, at least it's staying on your body. For now."

"I want to go on. I must go on," Dave chanted, as if it was his new mantra.

"Don't forget to mention our sponsors. The Eton Campaign Casino Night," Annie reminded him, slapping his shoulders like a trainer might warm up a boxer.

Haley checked the focus on the camera and centered Dave in the frame. "I really don't agree with this," she said. "But we're evidently going live in five, four, three . . ." She pointed at Dave as a signal to begin. He just sat there, dripping sweat on his plaid shirt.

"Dave!" she whispered. "Go!"

He should be used to this by now, Haley thought. Yes, this was his first videocast, but he'd been doing podcasts for years. Maybe nerves weren't the problem—or not the only problem. Dave's eyes were glazed, his pupils huge. Too much studying and not enough sleep had taken a serious toll.

"Am I on? Hello out there in video land." Dave stared into the camera, then giggled. "Video land. Where is that magic place? Out there, out there, somewhere. Where you are!" He pointed at the camera. Then he stared at his finger as if it were speaking to him. "What's that, finger? Stop pointing you? Sorry." He dropped his hand to his side and screamed. Or more like scream-barked: *"Arf! Arf-arf!"*

"Oh my god," Annie gasped. "What's he doing?"

"He's losing it," Haley said. "Should we cut him off?"

"We can't," Annie said. "It's his show. Besides, he'll never let us."

Dave looked up at the ceiling, then whipped his head around. "Did you see that? Did you people see that? I think it was a shadow person. Have you heard about the shadow people? They're gray, and small, and they sneak up on you while you're sleeping and suck your life force away. But they can't get me, because I never sleep! That'll show them! Come and get me, you little gray two-dimensional aliens!"

"This is a disaster," Haley said. "Dave!" she whispered. "Focus! Think Hillsdale, school—what's your topic today?"

"What? Oh, right. The topic of the day is . . . it's . . . um . . ."

"Getting into college," Annie prompted. "SAT prep and all that."

"No, no." Dave shook his head. "I don't want to talk about that. I want to talk about my trip to outer space. I saw the stars up close, and do you know what they looked like? Broken glass. Really, really shiny broken glass, with a number on each shard, and the numbers form a code. . . ."

By the next morning, Dave's videocast appeared to be a huge success. His regular audience had tuned in, and when they saw the fiasco, they'd texted all their friends and told them to watch "Serious 'n' Delirious" Dave's meltdown live on the Net. Soon clips of his show were circulating through in-boxes all over Hillsdale and beyond. People couldn't get enough of it. By the next morning at school, he'd gotten over fifty thousand hits. When Haley saw a girl walk by with a *Late Night with Madman Metzger* sticker on her school binder, she knew Dave's cult following was cemented. And she was pretty certain Annie was not going to be happy with all the negative attention her boyfriend had garnered overnight. What would all the admissions officers think?

● ● ●

Dave's videocast was quite the comedy sketch, only the joke was on him. Has Dave really gone postal? Too much studying and not enough sleep can wreak havoc on the best minds—and all the studying in the world won't help Dave's grades if his brain stops working. How will Dave react to the demands of his online peers for more Madman Metzger and Serious 'n' Delirious Dave? And how does Annie feel about all the people tuning in to poke fun at her boyfriend? Does Dave even realize people aren't laughing *with* him?

If you think Haley should stick around to help Dave deal with his newfound fame, go to page 242 (FIGHTING WORDS). If, on the other hand, you think she's had enough of Dave and Annie's overdrive craziness and needs a little fun herself, send her to CASINO NIGHT on page 248.

Sometimes you've just got to roll with the punch lines.

TALKING TRASH

Once an insult's been hurled, you can't ever take it back.

Haley left Whitney's house with her head so packed with gossip she felt physically dizzy. So many juicy rumors! She was full to bursting with them. The next day at school, when she bumped into Annie Armstrong and Annie asked her if she'd been to Whitney's new house yet, what was Haley supposed to do? Not tell her that Sasha's dad was getting ready to propose to Whitney's mom, turning the two former friends/now enemies into stepsisters? Haley couldn't deprive Annie of news like that. And the dish about

Mia's potential hookup video? Icing on the cake, which Annie lapped up and immediately spread all over Hillsdale.

By the next morning, Haley sensed the buzzing of chatter all over town. She heard her mother mention the rumors on the phone with Annie's mom before breakfast. She heard the kids on the bus whispering. And when she got to school, the first thing she saw was Whitney running out of the girls' bathroom in tears, her mascara raccooning her eyes.

"I can't take it!" Whitney wailed as she pushed against the stream of kids flooding the hallways. "If one more person asks me about my messed-up family, I'm transferring to Ridgewood!"

"Whitney!" Haley called out. She started to go after her to try to undo some of the damage, but the look Whitney gave her was so angry it clearly was a lost cause. She let Whitney go and find someone else's shoulder to cry on.

The buzzing continued, the whispers in the halls and classrooms growing to a roar. On the way to gym, someone called Haley's name. "Haley Miller!" the girl yelled in a Spanish accent. "I want to talk to you!"

Mia Delgado strode down the hall like a leopard, easily catching up with Haley. Haley stopped, but when she saw the look in Mia's eyes, she knew running would have been the safer option.

"You!" Mia shouted, shoving Haley against a wall

of lockers. "Why? Why you telling everybody lies about me? Huh? You jealous? Why?"

"They're not lies," Haley said, peeling herself off the lockers and charging at Mia. "They're true!"

"What do *you* know?" Mia cried. "You know nothing about me." She shoved Haley again. Haley shoved back, and Mia pushed her until she tumbled to the ground. The two of them rolled around on the hall floor, wrestling, pulling each other's hair and screaming.

"Go Mia! Go Mia!" some of the kids chanted.

"Take her top off!" a boy shouted.

"What's going on here?" a gym teacher demanded, prying the two girls apart. Haley leaned against the wall, panting and spitting hair out of her mouth.

"*Ho-la,* Mia," Haley said, purposely mispronouncing the Spanish word. "Emphasis on the *ho.*"

"What happened?" the gym teacher asked.

"Why don't you ask her?" Haley said, getting to her feet. "She started it."

Both girls were sent directly to Principal Crum's office, and by the time he heard the eyewitness accounts and saw Mia's cuts and scrapes for himself, Haley was suspended from school. No one who knew the circumstances was surprised.

● ● ●

What was Haley thinking, talking trash? Since when does she stoop to the level of catfights and gossip? She should have known better than to spread rumors— especially Coco-fueled ones. Mia was badly bruised from the spat, but the only person Haley permanently hurt was herself. With a suspension on her record, Haley's impeccable transcript was tarnished. Forever.

Hang your head and go back to page 1.

Spreading rumors is almost never a good idea.

The following day, Haley decided to go home straight after school. With all the trash talk floating around, she thought it best to steer clear and tune out. Haley was never one to spread rumors, so why should she start now?

"Hey Mom, I'll be up in my room," Haley called into the kitchen as she arrived home, then immediately darted upstairs. She definitely didn't want to talk to anyone this afternoon, and that included her mother, who, thanks to Annie Armstrong's mom, now seemed to know a little too much about the comings and goings of Hillsdale residents.

As Haley closed the bedroom door behind her, she sighed with relief. It was good to finally be alone, safe from idle chatter. She logged on to her computer and started to write a blog entry, which she entitled "The High Road Less Taken."

> Sometimes girls annoy me. You don't hear boys talking behind each other's backs and saying rude things about each other. How lame would it be if Spencer Eton was telling everyone at school that Drew Napolitano had gotten a little chubby this football season and was now purging in the bathroom to get rid of the extra weight?
>
> What is it with rumors? Who starts them anyway? And why do we feel the need to pass them along? For the sake of other people's entertainment? My Gram Polly would say "any friend who talks behind your back isn't your friend in the first place," and I have to admit, I think she's right.

Satisfied that she had successfully removed herself from Coco's vicious gossip cycle, at least for one day, Haley hit Post. She wasn't changing the world, but at least she wasn't making it any worse.

• • •

Good for Haley. Her refusal to be a pawn in Coco's gossip game probably saved her a heap of trouble. The question is, what should Haley do next? If you think she's strong enough to handle any temptations Coco and her crowd can dish out and still have a good time, send her to CASINO NIGHT on page 248. If you think she should keep her distance from Coco's campaigning, forget about the rumor mill and focus on leading the Hillsdale soccer team to victory, go to page 260 (SHOW SOME MERCY).

When you're feeling tempted, making the right choice takes serious discipline. Like turning-down-hot-chocolate-chip-cookies-right-out-of-the-oven discipline.

PRINCIPAL CRUM'S LITANY

If you don't want your house robbed, don't go handing out keys.

"I hear whispers in these hallowed halls about deviant initiation rituals on our sports teams," Principal Crum barked as Haley slipped into the auditorium. "There's talk of unmentionable behavior being recorded and broadcast on the World Wide Interweb. And no, I'm not talking about the 'Inside Hillsdale' videocast." Haley took a seat in the back and looked around for familiar faces. The entire school was there, or mostly there.

She spotted Irene, Shaun and Devon across the

aisle. They all three were covered in paint—Haley assumed they'd been working on the sets for *A Midsummer Night's Dream*. Shaun was taking his role as Bottom quite seriously, and had taken to wearing his costume to school. Today, mercifully, he had set his donkey head on the seat next to him. Shaun still whispered *hee-haw* every time Principal Crum said something funny, however, causing Devon and Irene to burst into muffled giggles.

Spencer was apparently cutting the assembly, but Coco, Whitney, Cecily and Mia sat together in a middle row, with Sebastian just behind them whispering into Mia's ear. A few rows to the left, Annie and Hannah sat looking dazed and trying hard to focus on the speech. Dave was with them—his head lolling on his neck as if he couldn't quite hold it up. His foot kept nervously *tap-tap-tap*ping on the floor. The college-prep pressure seemed to be getting to all three of them, which was a shame, Haley thought. If anyone had a great shot at getting into a good school, it should have been the brain-trust trio of Annie, Dave and Hannah.

The kids sitting around them were all watching Dave intently, as if expecting him to do or say something funny. He didn't disappoint. Every once in a while he quietly barked, or pointed at the ceiling with a terrified expression, as if he'd just spotted a team of ninjas attacking from the roof.

Poor Dave, Haley thought. He'd taken his podcast,

"Inside Hillsdale," to video, where the whole world could see how beyond-stressed-out he was. The camera recorded—and sent out into cyberspace—his every nutty utterance. The students of Hillsdale thought the show was a riot and passed clips of the video to all their friends. Dave Metzger had only enhanced his cult following, even if he was now a laughingstock.

"I'm taking these rumors seriously," Principal Crum said, "and because of this threat we are now on Burnt Sienna Alert."

A scattering of kids snickered at this.

"I am warning you all now," Principal Crum said. "The sports team captains will be held personally responsible for any mistreatment of their fellow students. If I hear a breath of a word about hazing or injuries, I will come after you and you will be sorry."

Haley heard rowdy thumps and rumbles overhead and craned her neck to look up into the balcony, which had been taken over by jocks of both sexes. Sasha and most of her soccer teammates were up there, along with Reese and the boys' team, and Drew and the football players. No sign of Johnny Lane. Haley hadn't seen him with Sasha much lately, but even if he deigned to attend an assembly like this, he probably wouldn't be up in the jock section, even though he was an ace basketball player.

Haley was surprised Reese had time to spare for an assembly. He'd been so busy studying the past few weeks Haley had hardly seen him, even though he lived right next door.

"We have had problems like this in the past," Principal Crum continued. "And rest assured, those who perpetrated the incidents were severely punished. Only a few years ago the tennis team set a flock of ducks loose in the cafeteria." There was scattered giggling from the students. "It was no laughing matter," Principal Crum said sternly. "Not only was it a serious health-code violation, but do you know I found duck feathers in my lunch for weeks afterward?"

Shaun yelled out a loud "quack!" to the amusement of everyone but Principal Crum.

"Even worse than that, ten years ago the football team locked a cow in my office overnight," he said. "You can imagine the kind of mess I found when I came in to work the next morning."

There was a collective *"Mooooo,"* from the stands. Everyone laughed.

"It's not funny, people!" Principal Crum shouted. "That year the entire football team was suspended. The captain lost his scholarship to Rutgers. And when the volleyball team filled the pool with red dye and a slashed-up dummy floating on its stomach, trust me, they too paid the price."

The jock crowd began stomping their feet, and Haley realized the principal's speech was backfiring. Instead of discouraging initiation rituals, he was actually inspiring teams to try to outdo the pranks of their predecessors. Crum was giving them ideas.

• • •

How clueless can Principal Crum get? Now the jocks are raging to initiate their newbies, and in their minds, thanks to the principal's harangue, it's a school tradition—practically their duty to uphold.

What does Haley think of all this? Does she want to become part of Hillsdale's illustrious history of hazing? Or is she more interested in other activities? Which group does Haley identify with these days? If you want to send Haley to hang with the jocks, go to page 255 (NEW JERSEY WATER TORTURE). If you think she'd like to see what Coco, Whitney and Mia have been up to, and how Mrs. Eton's gubernatorial campaign is going, place your bets on page 248 (CASINO NIGHT). If you think Haley is more into the drama scene these days, go to page 264 (COME ON, IRENE). Finally, if you want to give Haley's love life a jolt, go to page 242 (FIGHTING WORDS).

With colleges looking closely at junior year transcripts, Haley's decisions are becoming ever more important—from the friends she chooses to the extracurricular activities she participates in and the time she spends studying. Will she blow her chances and have a little fun? Or will she chicken out and play it safe?

INITIATION

Make sure you know what you're getting into before you sign up for the initiation.

"I think Leah and Marissa would be disappointed if we didn't initiate them," Haley said, referring to the two freshman players who had just made the girls' varsity soccer team. Haley and Sasha, cocaptains, had gotten together at Drip after school to come up with an initiation scheme.

"You're right," Sasha said. "It will make them feel like part of the group. Plus, the other girls are dying to do it."

"Please. They're just glad they're not the ones being hazed," Haley said.

"To be honest, so am I," Sasha said.

"Maybe we should make them be guests on Dave Metzger's videocast," Haley said. "Have you seen the clips of that thing?"

Supernerd Dave Metzger's "Inside Hillsdale" podcast had recently gone video, which was maybe not the best idea Dave had ever come up with. The junior-year-transcript pressure cooker was known to fell even the hardiest straight-A student. Dave was no exception. He was already so obsessed with applying to college next year, the unraveling had begun. During the videocast, Dave seemed to be hallucinating, sweating and spewing strange non sequiturs. Weirdly, the show was even more popular than his faceless podcast had been—the whole school thought his sweaty meltdown was hilarious.

"Someone forwarded me the footage," Sasha said. "So bizarre. I don't think we should let our frosh anywhere near that train wreck."

"You're probably right," Haley said. "There's a big pep rally coming up next week. We could make them wear their bras and panties on the outside of their clothes during the whole rally. Maybe even streak across the stage."

"I don't know," Sasha said. "Embarrass them in front of the whole school like that? It's also way too risky. Principal Crum could turn up. Maybe we should keep the initiation just between us. What about a banana-eating contest? Make them race to see which one can eat the most bananas in the fastest time. We did that at a slumber party at Coco's in eighth grade. It was pretty funny."

Haley sighed. Do something Sasha'd done in eighth grade? It just didn't seem cool enough. "Maybe we should get the boys involved—make the initiation coed. We are, after all, all Hillsdale soccer players, boys *and* girls. We could use more spirit on both sides."

"But whatever we do to Leah and Marissa will be that much more embarrassing if boys are there," Sasha said.

"And that's a bad thing?" Haley asked mischievously.

● ● ●

Are Haley and Sasha really going through with this coed initiation? It could be fun, unless you're a member of the freshman class. Maybe it really will shore up team spirit, but what if something goes wrong? Adding boys into the mix could stir up a dangerous cocktail. Haley's decision is up to you.

If you want the girls' team to join the boys for a coed initiation ritual, go to page 255 (NEW JERSEY WATER TORTURE). If you think Haley's having second thoughts and wants to take it easy on the younger girls, turn to page 260 (SHOW SOME MERCY). Finally, if you think Haley should forget initiation and check in with Annie and Alex at debate team practice, go to page 242 (FIGHTING WORDS).

It is always wise to trust your instincts. If something doesn't feel right, it probably isn't.

RUN LINES WITH DEVON

The dramas of real life
have a way of spilling over
onto the stage.

"Let's do that scene again," Devon said. He and Haley were sitting behind the cluttered counter at Jack's Vintage Clothing one afternoon, studying their copies of *A Midsummer Night's Dream*. The store where Devon worked was always pretty quiet in the afternoons, so he had invited Haley there to rehearse with him.

"Really?" Haley asked. "I thought we had it down last time. Shouldn't we move on?"

"Sure, you know the lines," Devon said. "But do you feel them?"

"Uh-oh, you're starting to sound like Shaun," Haley said.

They'd practiced this particular scene together over and over, and Haley was beginning to feel tired. She was amazed that Devon wanted to keep going—but kind of pleased by it too. Reading the part of Demetrius seemed to loosen him up a little, and it wasn't exactly a chore to do love scenes with him.

"You know what Xavier says," Devon said. "You have to *become* Helena. You have to feel what she feels. Let's do it one more time."

"Okay," Haley said. She closed her eyes and took a deep breath. She didn't even need to look at her script anymore. "You start."

Devon read Demetrius's lines: " 'If thou follow me, do not believe / But I shall do thee mischief in the wood.' "

" 'Ay, in the temple, in the town, the field,' " Haley/Helena said.

> " 'You do me mischief. Fie, Demetrius!
> Your wrongs do set a scandal on my sex:
> We cannot fight for love, as men may do;
> We should be woo'd and were not made to
>   woo.
> I'll follow thee and make a heaven of hell,
> To die upon the hand I love so well.' "

Haley, whose character, Helena, loved Demetrius to the point of obsession, gazed lovingly and longingly at Devon's face. In character, of course. She stared into Devon's eyes and was startled to find him gazing at her with affection, too.

"Uh, Demetrius, hello? You don't love Helena yet. At this point you still think she's a pest."

"Oh." Devon looked away. "Right. Helena's really bonkers over me. I can't stand her. Got it."

"If you ask me, she takes things a little too far," Haley added. "But at least she gets her man in the end."

"Let's do that part," Devon said suddenly. "That last bit at the end of act four, scene one. We'll start at 'And all the faith . . .'"

Haley checked her script and waited for her cue. Devon declaimed,

"'And all the faith, the virtue of my heart,
The object and the pleasure of mine eye,
Is only Helena. To her, my lord,
Was I betroth'd ere I saw Hermia:
But, like in sickness, did I loathe this food;
But, as in health, come to my natural taste,
Now I do wish it, love it, long for it,
And will for evermore be true to it.'"

"'And I have found Demetrius like a jewel,'" Haley said. "'Mine own, and not mine own.'"

" 'It seems to me,' " Devon said, " 'That yet we sleep, we dream.' "

His eyes were shining, and Haley could see that he was totally caught up in the moment when Demetrius realizes at last that he loves his Helena. Devon leaned close to her and pressed his lips on hers in a tender kiss.

Haley kissed him back. This was how Helena would kiss her Demetrius—all out, with passion. Soon they were making out like two wild forest nymphs. They were so into each other Haley didn't hear the door open or someone walking up to the counter.

"Ew!" Whitney cried, staring in horror at their on the clock make-out session. "Get a room!"

Haley and Devon broke apart, panting and red-faced. Devon straightened his tweed vest and restored his pageboy hat to his head. "Can I help you?" he asked.

"Not if it involves cramming your tongue down my throat," Whitney whined. "But yes, I do need something. Do you think I'd set foot in this moth hatchery otherwise?"

"Well, what is it?" Devon asked.

"I need to see some seventeenth-century corsets, quickly," Whitney said. "Where do you keep them?"

"Real seventeenth-century corsets?" Devon said. "We don't carry that kind of vintage."

"What do you need them for?" Haley asked. "Is this for the play? You are doing our costumes, right?"

"Actually, this is for a dress I'm making for Mrs. Eton's Casino Night fund-raiser," Whitney said. "A corset would make this perfect body even more perfecter."

"We do have a Madonna-inspired corset on aisle three," Devon said. "It's not from the seventeenth century, obviously, but it might work for your dress."

"Thank you." Whitney stomped over to aisle three to find the corset. "Try to keep your clothes on until I leave, please," she called out to them.

Haley blushed. Devon pulled her close and whispered, "That was fun."

"We got a little carried away there. Maybe we were too much in character."

"I can't tell the difference between me and Demetrius anymore," Devon admitted. "I almost called you Helena the other day, and we weren't even rehearsing."

Whitney returned with the corset, eyeing both of them suspiciously. "Okay," she said. "I'll take it."

Devon rang it up and put it in a bag for her; then Whitney was out the door.

Devon turned to Haley. "You know who's really taking this acting thing to the far side, of course."

"Who?" Haley asked.

"Shaun and Irene."

"Oh, I know," Haley said. "The whole donkey thing."

"It's worse than you think," Devon said. "You know what they've been doing after rehearsals?"

"What?!" Haley demanded, strangely fascinated.

"Shaun puts on his donkey head and makes Irene ride on his back while he hee-haws and tries to buck her off."

Haley was stunned.

"Really? I can't see Irene going for that," she said.

"Are you kidding?" Devon said. "She acts all snarky and cool, but Shaun tells me she's a wild woman in private."

He leaned in to give her another kiss. Haley kissed him back, but then pulled away. She couldn't get the disturbing image of Irene and Donkey Shaun out of her mind. Would Irene really be into something so bizarre? Haley wasn't sure she believed Devon. Maybe it was only gossip. Then again, maybe it wasn't.

●　●　●

It's not like Devon to gossip—is it? He's suddenly opened up to Haley, a lot. Must be all this role-playing, and the stimulating effect of Shakespeare. But did he see Irene riding on Shaun's back with his own eyes? If so, Haley might need to have a talk with Irene. Everyone seems to be losing their marbles these days.

If you think Haley should see what's going on with Irene and her set design for the school play, go to page 264 (COME ON, IRENE). If you think Irene is a lost cause and Haley's time would be better spent in the world of politics, send her off to party with Coco, Whitney and the country club set at CASINO NIGHT on page 248.

In a small town like Hillsdale, it's hard to keep a secret. Haley'd best make sure she has nothing to hide.

FIGHTING WORDS

What you don't know
can hurt you.

"Dave is practically catatonic," Annie said as she and Haley headed into debate team practice. *Well, you don't look so hot yourself,* Haley thought, noticing that Annie's hair was scraggly and unwashed, and she'd clearly chewed her nails ragged.

"Half the time he doesn't even make sense," Annie went on. "Something's terribly wrong. Unless, he's gotten so brilliant that I can't follow his train of thought anymore. But no—what am I saying? That's just not possible. I'm Annie Armstrong."

"Does seem unlikely," Haley said. They took their seats in the debate room and waited for Annie's cocaptain, Alex, to arrive. Haley sat next to Dale Smithwick, a tall, skinny African American boy with round glasses.

"Let's face it," Annie said. "Dave's just gone loco."

"I'll say," said Dale.

"Why? Have you been watching his videocast?" Annie asked.

"Not exactly," Dale said. "One of my friends e-mailed me some clips—hilarious. Better than stand-up. Last episode, Dave was talking to the ghost of his dead hamster. Which I think he named Handel?"

"The dude is seriously messed up," another debater chimed in. "He's all, 'I'd like to tell you what Handel says about the afterlife, but first I must translate from the original Hamster.' "

"You mean—" Annie looked upset. "These clips are bouncing around the Internet like comedy sketches?"

"Totally," Dale said. "I've got a friend in Georgia who keeps begging me to send him more. Dave's famous."

"A famous nut job," the other boy added.

"This is terrible!" Annie exclaimed.

"Come on, Annie," Dale prodded. "You must have seen this coming. Dave is airing those videocasts twice a week. Do you think nobody's watching? How can you not find that stuff funny?"

"Poor Dave," Annie said absently. "If he knew everyone was laughing at him—"

"Get your boyfriend a good shrink and an even better dermatologist," Dale recommended.

"You're one to talk," Haley said, pointing to the spotty breakout on Dale's chin.

Just then, Alex Martin walked in and took his place at the front of the room. "Let's get started, everyone. We've got a big debate with St. Agnes next week and we don't want to ruin our stellar one-and-zero record."

He flashed Haley a quick grin, causing her pulse to quicken. She loved Alex's smart, take-charge personality, and his preppy adorableness didn't hurt. While they had gotten off to a rocky—okay, practically violent—start, sparks were definitely now flying between them. They tried to keep things cool during debate team practices, since Haley didn't think it would be a good idea to broadcast their serious flirtation to the other debaters—didn't want to provoke any accusation of favoritism. But it was getting harder and harder to be in a room together without locking eyes.

"The topic will be technology and whether it is improving our lives," Alex said. "I want everyone to practice arguing both pro and con, so we'll be ready for anything St. Aggie throws at us. Let's start with Annie taking pro against Dale's con—"

Suddenly, the classroom door flew open and

Sebastian Bodega stormed in. "Haley!" he shouted. "I must speak to you."

"Excuse me, Sebastian," Alex said. "We're in the middle of debate practice."

"It is very important," Sebastian said. He fell onto his knees in front of Haley. "It cannot wait another moment."

"I'm sorry?" Alex began, glancing at Haley with a confused look.

"Haley, please, I beg of you," Sebastian said, taking her hand.

"Um, maybe I should talk to him in the hall." Haley wondered what on earth Sebastian might want. They'd barely exchanged more than a few pleasantries this school year, he'd been so busy with Mia.

Alex looked to Annie for her opinion, as if Annie could stop this unpleasant interruption. She just shrugged.

"Five minutes," Alex said sternly. "We can't spare any more than that."

"Oh, thank you," Sebastian said. "Haley, come."

Haley followed Sebastian into the hall. "Sebastian, this better be good—"

"Oh, Haley, I am so sorry," Sebastian began. "For anything I ever put you through. Each time Mia, she does something to me, she pierces my heart, I think this is what I have done to Haley. And it kills me that I have put you through such pain."

"Actually," Haley said, a bit taken aback, "I haven't really given you much thought in months."

"Don't speak, my precious. Your suffering is too great for me to bear. I must spend my life now trying to make this up to you."

"What about Mia?" Haley asked.

"Mia, Mia, Mia. No matter how many times I tell people she is my EX-girlfriend, no one believes me."

"Maybe that's because you two are always hanging all over each other," Haley offered. Though truthfully, in Mia's case, she was always hanging all over a lot of boys.

"We are Espanish," he said. "Hot-blooded, romantic people. We are expressive. We touch! Is no big thing."

"So you interrupted debate practice just to tell me all that?"

"No," Sebastian said. "I must, I need, to tell you that I truly still care for you, Haley. I want to be with you. Won't you please say you want to be with me also?"

● ● ●

Well, this is a surprise. Who knew Sebastian was pining for Haley all this time? But is Haley willing to give him another try? He sure seems to want her back—for now. Can she trust him? His feelings in the past have been all over the map. "Hot-blooded" is right—there have been times when Sebastian has seemed to be hot for every

girl he saw. But he just made such a dramatic gesture, bursting in and declaring his feelings.... Maybe he really means it this time.

Then there's Alex. It feels as though things are heating up with him, and Haley hasn't had a chance to see where it will lead. If she goes back to Sebastian, she'll have to drop Alex. And something tells her that Alex, unlike Sebastian, won't come running back to her if things with Señor Bodega don't work out.

What should Haley do? Pursue Alex or Sebastian? Or neither? Or both? If you think Haley should jump at the chance to tango with the Spanish Hottie, go to page 267 (BODEGA'S BOLOGNA). If you think stable, reliable Alex is the best bet for Haley, send her on a DATE WITH ALEX on page 270. Or, if you're not ready to commit just yet, INVESTIGATE MIA on page 273. Finally, if you think Haley should start paying more attention to her test preparations, go to page 285 (TESTING LIMITS).

Just like on multiple-choice exams, if you don't know the answer, you've still got to pick one and move on.

When you roll around in the mud, expect to get dirty.

"**W**hat's the problem here?" Perry Miller asked. He'd walked into the kitchen after dinner to find Joan and Haley arguing while Mitchell took apart the microwave. Haley was dressed up in a short shift dress, the charcoal fabric shimmering with sparkly silver thread. She wore her auburn hair in a loose updo, and silver pumps on her feet.

"She wants to go to that ridiculous fund-raiser," Joan said, pointing at her daughter. "For a Republican!"

"She won't drive me," Haley said, pointing back at her mom.

Spencer Eton's mother was having a Casino Night at their palatial home, and Spencer had invited the cream of Hillsdale High to attend. Haley knew her mother couldn't stand Mrs. Eton's environmentally unfriendly political platform, but she didn't think Joan would ruin her social life just because she didn't agree with the Eton values.

"I would hate to support anything that woman does," Joan said. "And I can't stand to think of my own daughter wallowing in that political pigpen. I also don't understand why a bunch of sixteen-year-olds need to hang around at a party full of conservative grown men and women anyway. It's like they're trying to indoctrinate the next generation!"

"Look, I don't agree with Mrs. Eton's politics either," Haley said. "But I'm not giving her campaign any money. If anything, I'm costing them dollars by getting a free seat and eating their food."

Tickets to Casino Night were $1,500 a pop, but Spencer had put his friends, including Haley, on the guest list, gratis.

"Your presence alone is a show of support," Joan said.

"Dad, I'm only going because all my friends will be there," Haley said. "For me it's just a party, not a political showdown."

Perry looked warily from his wife to his daughter

and back. "I'll drive you, honey," he said to Haley finally.

"Fine," Joan seethed, storming out of the room. "As long as *I'm* not compromising my conscience." She stomped up the stairs.

"Look," Mitchell said, pressing a button on the reconfigured microwave. "I can make the clock run backward. It's the first step in building a machine that will be able to take me back in time."

"Just don't take us back to the era when you talked like a robot," Haley teased, pulling on her coat. She felt mildly guilty for going against her own mother. But she also loved the sensation of winning an argument.

"Mitchell, could you have the clock running forward again by the time I get back?" Perry said. "I'm sure you're capable of making a time machine, but I don't think this family can handle interruptions in the space-time continuum right now."

"No problem," Mitchell said.

Perry drove Haley to the Etons', dropping her off in the circular drive behind a line of cars queued up for valet-parking service. The mansion was aglow; music and laughter poured from its windows.

"Have a good time, honey," Perry said. "I'll try to cool your mother down before you get home."

"Thanks, Dad. Just tell her I'm sabotaging the system from the inside." Haley gave him a quick kiss and hopped out of the car.

The party was packed, mostly with well-dressed adults, but a few clusters of glamorous teens sparkled among the crowd. Most of the action was in the casino, set up in the huge living room. Waiters floated by with trays of drinks and jewel-like canapés while the adults played roulette and black-jack.

Definitely the work of Spencer, Haley thought as she surveyed the scene. Spencer Eton had plenty of experience setting up gambling parties with the help of his SIGMA pals, and this one had his signature touches: good-looking people and very high stakes. The event looked to be a huge hit for Mrs. Eton.

Just then, Spencer came over to greet her, with Coco on his arm and Whitney teetering behind them on gold high heels.

"Now I can really say everybody in Hillsdale who counts is here," Spencer said, kissing Haley on the cheek.

"I thought you were allergic to bleeding-heart liberals," Haley teased.

"If we don't open our doors to our misguided friends, how can we ever convert them to the truth?" Spencer retorted.

"My dad used to be a Democrat," Whitney confessed. "He switched parties a few years back. Something about the tax rate. He's here . . . some-where. . . ." She looked around for her dad, Jerry Klein, the breath-spray king of New Jersey. "Trish stayed home to watch reality TV, so I'm his date tonight."

"If you can find him," Coco said.

"Truth is power, Haley," Spencer said. "And vice versa. You have to use whatever power you've got. There's political power, social power, financial and . . . the other kind." Haley followed his eyes toward the front door, where Mia Delgado was making a splashy entrance in a short, spangled low-cut dress and heels so high she towered over most of the men in the room.

Whitney looked down at her own curve-hugging satin dress and wailed, "Why do I even bother?"

Actually, Haley thought, *Whitney's dress is especially flattering.* But she knew what Whitney meant—it was hard to get any attention with Mia sucking the air out of every room she entered.

"What's she doing here?" Coco demanded. "She wasn't on the guest list."

"Maybe she should have been. We should go say hello," Spencer said, leading Coco away. Whitney followed without being invited, while Haley headed for the bar to get a plain soda. The kids were under strict orders not to drink, lest some tabloid snap a photo and accuse Mrs. Eton of serving minors in her own home.

As Haley wandered through the crowd, checking out the games, she came across Mrs. Eton holding forth to a cluster of guests.

"Are you enjoying yourselves?" Mrs. Eton was saying. "People love gambling—it's part of human nature, isn't it? When I'm governor I'm going to bring more gambling to the great state of New Jersey—more casinos, bigger lotteries . . . Gambling brings in so much revenue you can lower taxes to next to nothing."

One of her listeners, a large, red-faced man, nodded vigorously. "Lower taxes, that's what it's all about," he said. "You've got the vote of everyone in the Heights if you promise to lower taxes."

If Mom were here she'd cause a riot, Haley thought, grateful Joan was safe at home under lock and key. Haley moved away from the candidate's circle and spotted an odd couple isolated in a back corner of the room.

Mia Delgado leaned against the wall, laughing with delight at something the man with her had said. The man was stocky and middle-aged, with a bald spot on the back of his head. Mia leaned close and whispered something, touching his shoulder.

She was flirting. But with whom? Haley moved closer for a better look.

The man brushed Mia's long hair from her collarbone. Then he turned slightly and nodded toward the bar. At last Haley could see his face.

It was Jerry Klein.

Haley couldn't believe it. Mia was flirting with Whitney's dad!

Holy guacamole! Mia and Whitney's dad? What exactly is going on here? Haley doesn't want to jump to conclusions—or does she? Mia seems to have a voracious need to conquer every male who crosses her path. Who's she going to flirt with next, Mitchell?

And how did she get into the fund-raiser in the first place? She wasn't on Spencer's guest list, and Haley doubted Mia could spare $1,500 to support a candidate in an election she couldn't even vote in. Yet here she was. Mia certainly seemed to have a knack for being in the right place at the right time.

If you think Haley should find out what's going on between Mia and Mr. Klein, go to page 273 (INVESTIGATE MIA). Or if you want Haley to wait for more information before she jumps to conclusions, go to page 277 (INCURABLE FLIRT). If you think Haley should leave this lions' den altogether and attend to her own personal life, and perhaps a cute senior who has a crush on her, send her on a DATE WITH ALEX on page 270. Finally, if you think she misses Reese and would rather try to reconcile with him, go to page 302 (WATCH AND LEARN).

As Spencer said, there are different kinds of power. One type he didn't mention: willpower.

NEW JERSEY WATER
TORTURE

You can lead a frosh to water, and you can make her drink.

"Hey, boys, what's on the agenda?" Haley asked as she and Sasha led the girls' varsity soccer team through the front door of Zach Woolsey's house for the first unofficial coed initiation. Zach was a senior on the boys' team, who lived in the Heights. He wasn't a captain on the boys team, but he'd offered to step in and host when Reese had predictably bailed on the whole hazing idea. It looked as though the boys had already gotten the party started. Their three freshmen were sitting at a table with six huge jugs of water in front of them.

"Gulp it down!" Zach said, forcefully. "We're making them drink at least a gallon of water each," he explained to the girls. "These frosh are going to be up all night pissing their pants."

"*That's* your initiation ritual?" Sasha said.

"It's better than watching them puke all night from drinking," Zach replied. "Or making them eat brownies laced with laxatives. The idiot lacrosse players tried that last year. You would not believe the mess."

"Well, what's good enough for the boys . . . ," Haley said, pulling up two chairs. "Leah and Marissa, looks like you've got some water to drink."

Haley gave them each a jug. The rest of the team seemed to be waiting for her to tell them what to do. It felt cool being in charge, having the power to boss the girls around. It was a new sensation for Haley, and one she instantly liked.

Marissa and Leah, the two freshman players, tilted their heads back and drank the water. After a few minutes of gulping, Marissa wiped her mouth. "My stomach's full. I can't drink any more."

Haley frowned. "Jen, check the jug to see how much she's had so far." Jen was a senior—so even seniors were following Haley's orders. Which was kind of awesome.

"She's only finished about half," Jen said.

"Keep going, Marissa," Haley demanded.

"How are you doing, Leah?" Sasha asked, looking a tad concerned.

Leah gulped and took a breath. "Okay."

"Come on, let's get some team spirit going!" Haley said. "Chug! Chug! Chug!"

The other girls followed along, chanting and cheering. "Chug! Chug! Chug!"

Marissa stopped and clutched her stomach. "Maybe we should let them take a break," Sasha suggested.

"What do you think, team?" Haley asked. "The boys aren't getting any breaks."

The other girls shouted, "Chug!"

By the end of the evening, Marissa and Leah had finished more than a gallon each. "Good job," Haley said, putting her arms around the two freshmen. "You are now official Lady Hawks. Congratulations."

"Ugh," Marissa groaned.

"My stomach," Leah said.

"My head," Marissa said, rubbing her temples.

"Come on, you guys will be fine," Haley said. "It's just water, right?"

The party broke up. Haley felt good as Sasha drove her home. "I think the girls had a good time, don't you?" she said.

"Yeah, except for Leah and Marissa."

Just then, Haley's cell buzzed. She glanced at the screen. Leah's name came up.

"Leah, what's up?"

"This isn't Leah. This is her mother. Leah and Marissa are both in the emergency room. Leah tells me Marissa passed out cold in the car on the way home. Just what were you girls doing tonight?"

"What's wrong with Marissa?" Haley asked, fear creeping into her voice.

"We don't know yet," Leah's mother said. "The doctors said something about water poisoning. But why would that be? You girls didn't have a game today."

The next day at school, the news was out. Marissa had gone into shock. Her system had been so overloaded with water it upset the saline balance in her blood. "The doctor said it was life-threatening. She could have died," Sasha told Haley after visiting the ER.

Haley's stomach hit the ground. This was bad. This was very bad. And it was about to get worse.

The word "life-threatening" sent the parents of Hillsdale into crisis mode, forcing the girls on the soccer team to confess what had happened. It wasn't long before Haley Miller was named as being the primary force behind the initiation stunt—it was her idea, the girls said. She made the freshmen drink.

That afternoon, Coach Tygert called Haley into his office. "I'm sorry to do this, Haley," he said. "But I have no choice but to strip you of your title as captain and kick you off the team."

"I thought it was safe," Haley protested. "I never heard that drinking too much water could be bad for you."

"You should never have forced your players to do something like this in the first place," Coach Tygert said. "Your job is to lead them, to help them, not send them to the hospital."

Haley was devastated and more humiliated than she'd ever been in her life. Just when she thought things couldn't get any worse, they did. Principal Crum expelled her. And then the local paper published an article about the cruel hazing incidents at Hillsdale High and named Haley Miller as one of the main perpetrators. Everyone shunned her. She became a pariah in town, friendless and alone.

● ● ●

How awful! Haley got carried away in her own initiation frenzy—with serious consequences. How could she treat her own teammates so cruelly? Even if she never thought too much water could be harmful, just causing them discomfort was bad enough. Is that any way for a captain to behave? Well, she's not the captain anymore, so that won't ever happen again. At least not on the girls' soccer team.

Hang your head and go back to page 1.

SHOW SOME MERCY

Sometimes leadership means taking one for the team.

By the time Haley got to Zach Woolsey's house in the Heights, the "initiation" process was already underway. Zach, a senior on the boys' soccer team, had agreed to a coed hazing, as long as the girls didn't wimp out. He wasn't a captain but had offered to host after Reese Highland had canceled at the last minute. It was no surprise that the minute the word *hazing* began to circulate, Reese had backed out.

Haley found her two freshmen, Leah and Marissa, sitting with the three frosh boys at a kitchen table loaded with huge jugs of water. Their teammates, boys and girls, surrounded them, ready to cheer them on.

"Now," Zach said. "I'm letting you frosh off easy. All you have to do is chug all the water on this table, and you're done. Initiated. Simple, right?"

"Not so fast," Haley said. This looked innocent enough, but she wasn't about to take any chances. Nothing bad would happen to her players, not on her watch. She took her position as captain of the team very seriously.

"Sorry, Zach, but my girls have already been initiated," she said, winking at Marissa and Leah. "They've been through the wringer, and I hate to make them suffer more. They don't deserve it. And actually, I think the rest of you freshman are going to end up on the team even if you don't drink the water. No one's going to fault you if you walk out right now."

"Come on," Zach said. "You promised you girls wouldn't wuss out."

"I don't remember making any promise like that," Haley said. "Come on, girls—time for pizza." She led her teammates out of the house with Sasha and saw all the freshman boys following them out the door.

"Thanks, Haley," Leah said once they arrived at Lisa's Pizza. "I really didn't want to drink all that water."

"Hazing is ridiculous," Haley declared. "Reese was right to have no part of that. Why would I want to abuse my own teammates? We've got a game in two days. It doesn't make sense."

A few girls were whispering at the other end of the table. "Hey, guys, did you hear about Mia Delgado?" asked one, her jaw dropping.

"What—more rumors about Mia?" Haley said. The new girl certainly knew how to get herself talked about, that was for sure.

"This is a doozy," Leah said. "I heard she went to that Casino Night fund-raiser at Spencer Eton's house—and was *flirting* with Whitney Klein's dad in front of everyone."

"You're kidding!" Haley said. "Mia? Are you sure? What would she see in Jerry Klein?"

"That's what I'd like to know," Sasha said. "That guy sure gets around."

Just then Haley's phone buzzed. She checked the screen: it was a text from Alex Martin, the cute senior head of the debate team.

"Would it be all right if I called you sometime?—Alex."

"What is it?" Sasha asked, looking at Haley's startled face.

"I think Alex Martin just asked me out."

"Nice," Sasha said, toasting Haley with her slice of pizza.

"Hey, do you want to go with me to pick up Johnny at Bubbies? I hate sitting there waiting alone.

And we can discuss how you're going to handle the cute senior with a crush on you."

● ● ●

What a busy night—in the best possible way. Haley kindly spared her frosh the ordeal of initiation. Who knows what could have happened? Protecting her teammates won her their undying loyalty and appreciation. For the rest of the season, they respected Haley's leadership more than ever.

But the decision making never ends. What's up with this rumor about Mia and Jerry Klein? Could it really be true? If you think Haley's curiosity about this mystery will not be slaked until she finds out the truth, send her to page 273 (INVESTIGATE MIA).

And then there's Alex's offer. Should she take him up on it and go out with him? What about Reese? Or the cute photographer Devon McKnight? Or Sebastian Bodega, for that matter? If Mia's flirty with Mr. Klein, does that mean her "Sebbie" is finally free? If you think Haley should give Alex a shot, go to page 270 (DATE WITH ALEX). If you think Haley should go to Bubbies with Sasha instead, turn to page 277 (INCURABLE FLIRT).

Haley's been on a roll lately, but should she keep rolling the dice?

COME ON, IRENE

Father does not always
know best.

"I've got some news," Irene announced. She and Haley were sitting in the courtyard eating lunch. "I'm quitting the play."

"What?" Haley was stunned. "But we need you! You're the most brilliant set designer ever! If you quit, the magical forest of Arden will look like a tumbleweed patch in Texas. Why are you quitting?"

"My parents, why else?" Irene said with a sigh. "They say the play takes up too much of my time. My grades are slipping again and I'm not working hard enough at the restaurant."

"That's ridiculous," Haley said. "You work harder than anyone I know. What did Shaun say?"

"I haven't told him yet. But I can guess what he'll say: 'Hee-haw, screw them.' "

"Irene, you are so talented," Haley said. "Your talent continually blows me away. But you can't let your parents control you so much. Stand up for yourself! You should be allowed to pursue the activities that interest you. How are you supposed to get into college if your only extracurricular is hostessing at a restaurant?"

"You don't understand," Irene said. "I can't reason with them. They believe children should never question their parents. Parents are always right."

"But they're not right this time, and you know it," Haley said. "You've got to stand up to them, Irene. Your future depends on it."

Irene paused. She seemed to really be taking what Haley was saying to heart.

"Fight for your right to paint," Haley added.

"Okay. I will."

Somehow, Haley wasn't sure if Irene really meant what she said.

● ● ●

Haley's taking a risk, getting involved in Irene's family life. Irene's parents have always been strict, but this time, in Haley's opinion, they've gone too far. But will Irene just get into more trouble if she takes Haley's advice?

If you think Haley should keep supporting Irene in her plea for independence and risk the wrath of Mr. Chen, go to page 281 (BASEMENT DWELLERS). If you think Haley should mind her own business, and that business should have something to do with the cute senior who is rumored to have a crush on her, Alex Martin, go to page 270 (DATE WITH ALEX).

Friends need all the support they can get—but butting into someone else's family life can cause a lot of trouble. Handle with care.

BODEGA'S BOLOGNA

You can't teach an old *perro* new tricks.

"I was so stupid to give you up," Sebastian said to Haley over lunch. "Look at you. Beautiful. A nice girl. Sensible. With a good head on her neck."

"You mean shoulders?" Not exactly the most romantic words Haley'd ever heard, but she'd take them.

"Did I say beautiful?" Sebastian grinned, his bright white teeth lighting up his gorgeous face.

"You can say that as many times as you want," Haley said. *Maybe I should give Sebastian another chance,* she thought. *He's so sexy, so romantic, so passionate, I'd be crazy not to jump all over this.*

"And you're smart too," Sebastian said. "Not like that crazy Mia. What a flirt! She cannot resist any man—she's always putting her hands all over them."

"Yeah, well, not everyone's as self-controlled and levelheaded as I am," Haley said, though she felt annoyed at the continued mention of Mia's name.

"She likes all the men, but especially the older men," Sebastian said. "I think that's wrong. Don't you?"

"Well, it's not the healthiest way to go through high school." Haley tried to keep the irritation out of her voice, but she was beginning to wonder whether this lunch was about her and Sebastian or Mia. He certainly seemed to think Mia was the more interesting topic of conversation.

"You would never do that to me, would you, Haley?" Sebastian said, caressing her hand. "You know how to behave with a boyfriend, not to throw yourself at every cheap bald man who offers you jewelry . . ."

● ● ●

Oops. When will Haley learn? Looks as though Haley got burned by the hot tamale once again. It's pretty obvious that Sebastian is still obsessed with Mia, and as far as he's concerned, Haley will always be second best.

Sebastian can't tame Mia, so he'll take Haley as a consolation prize? How selfish!

Haley may have been lured in by Sebastian's extremely toned swimmer's body and his suave charms, but she doesn't want to be anyone's alternate. She's going to have to forget about Sebastian and start over again.

Go back to page 1.

DATE WITH ALEX

What is written in the stars isn't always easy to make out from a distance.

"There's the Big Dipper." Alex pointed to a cup-shaped star formation on the planetarium ceiling. For their first official date, Alex had driven Haley into Manhattan and taken her to the planetarium at the Museum of Natural History. They sat inside the huge dome and gazed up at the stars. It was almost as romantic as lying in a field and watching the real night sky. Haley was duly impressed by how much Alex knew about astronomy.

"Those two stars at the front of the cup are called

pointers because they always point to the North Star," Alex said. "See it?"

Haley drew a line from the front of the Big Dipper to a bright star a few inches above it. "I see it. Cool."

"No matter where the Big Dipper is, whether it's upside down or in the west or east, it always points to the North Star," Alex said. "I love that about the universe. It's mysterious and strange, but also consistent. You can count on it. So now you'll always know which way north is."

"And I can never get lost again," Haley said. "Well, except during the daytime."

"Then you can use the sun," Alex reminded her.

"Not on cloudy days, though," Haley said, continuing to debate the ultimate debater.

"Well, I hope you never get lost," Alex said, relenting. "At least not so lost that I can't find you."

They sat together quietly for a minute, taking in the twinkling lights.

"Do you know the constellations?" Alex asked. "There's Libra. . . ."

At the mention of constellations, the California girl in Haley got the best of her. "What sign are you?" she asked.

Alex laughed. "Leo. It's that lion-shaped constellation up there. How about you?"

"Aquarius," she said. *Leo—yes!* she thought. She'd read that Leo and Aquarius were highly compatible—and the better she got to know Alex, the more she felt this was really true. "I'm an air sign," she said. "And Leo's fire."

"Fire needs air," Alex said. "Or it dies out. Isn't that how it goes? Not that I buy into any of that foolishness."

"I figured," Haley said. She turned her eyes away from the stars and caught him gazing at her face. Then he leaned close and kissed her.

"I've liked you from the moment I first noticed you lost in the math wing last year."

"Really?" Haley said. "You sure didn't act like it at first."

"I was playing hard to get," Alex teased.

"Well," said Haley, "I'm glad I gave you a chance."

"So am I," Alex replied.

He kissed her again, and she put her arms around him. Haley suddenly felt the urge to never let go. Alex was a senior, which meant he'd be off to college in just a few months, and they would have to make the best of the time they had. She gazed up, hoping this was only the first of many romantic liaisons under the stars. Alex's grip on her was every bit as tight, and she knew in that moment he felt exactly the same way.

THE END

It doesn't take a lot to shock
a small town.

"Do you think Mia just crashed Casino Night?" Haley said to Coco. "Not that I'd put anything past her, but crashing a political fund-raiser seems crazy even for her."

Coco had invited Haley to lunch at the country club. They sat outside on the terrace, basking in the last of the October sun. Haley wasn't sure what Coco wanted until the subject of Mia came up; then she understood.

"Did you see the security at the Etons' house?"

Coco said. "There's no way she crashed. And I saw Spencer's guest list—she wasn't on it."

"Someone must have *bought* her a ticket," Haley said. "But who?"

"I don't know," Coco said. "Although I have my suspicions. And I think I know how we can find out." She leaned forward and stared across the lawn toward the golf course. "Here she comes now."

"Who?" Haley saw a trim, familiar-looking woman in her twenties striding toward them in a golf skirt. A caddie trailed along behind her.

"Rachel," Coco said. "Mrs. Eton's social secretary."

So that was why the woman looked familiar, Haley thought. She must have seen Rachel at the Eton's soiree.

Coco summoned a waiter with a finger in the air. "Would you please ask Ms. Horton if she'd like to join us at our table for coffee?"

"Certainly, Miss De Clerq."

Fifteen minutes later, Rachel Horton appeared at their table carrying a gym bag and a briefcase. "Hello, Coco. Drinking coffee now? I thought you lived on the plasma of young boys."

Coco pretended to laugh through gritted teeth. "Rachel loves to tease," she said to Haley. "Rach, honey, I need a favor. Do you still have the guest lists from Casino Night?"

"I might," Rachel said. "But why should I do a favor for you?"

"Because if you don't," Coco said, "I'll tell Spencer I saw you and Garth canoodling at Bubbies the other night."

Rachel went pale.

"Who's Garth?" Haley asked.

"The campaign manager for Peter Welch, Mrs. Eton's biggest competitor," Coco said. "It doesn't look good when functionaries from rival campaigns fraternize, now, does it?"

"We were only exchanging messages," Rachel said. "Mrs. Eton offered to stop criticizing his health care policy if he stopped looking into Spencer's rap sheet."

"Sure you were," Coco said. "Through your tongues."

"Okay," Rachel said. "What do you want to know?"

"Look for the name Mia Delgado," Coco said. "I want to know whose guest list she was on."

Rachel opened her briefcase and riffled through her files. "Here it is. Mia Delgado. On the private guest list of Mr. Jerry Klein."

Haley gasped. "Whitney's father?"

"The very same," Coco said.

"Is that all?" Rachel asked.

"For now," Coco said. "You're dismissed."

Rachel closed her briefcase and left in a huff.

"Poor Whitney," Haley said. "Should we tell her?"

"I don't know," Coco said. "Would you want to

know, if it was *your* dad chasing around after a girl in our grade?"

● ● ●

What a dog. Haley couldn't imagine her dad behaving this way, which doesn't make it any easier to know what to do. It's hard for Haley to believe that Mia would flirt so shamelessly with someone's father. What does Mia want from Mr. Klein, anyway? Is she after something tangible, or is she just incapable of not flirting around the opposite sex? And what will Trish think of all this? After only a year, she's already being replaced?

If you think Whitney deserves to know the truth about her father, send Haley off to tell her on page 288 (HIGH SCHOOL HOME-WRECKER). If you think Haley should protect volatile Whitney's feelings and keep this to herself—and hope that Coco does the same—go to page 292 (CONCEALED WEAPON).

Even if Haley keeps this gossip to herself, there's no way of knowing what destructive Coco will do. If you think Haley should cut her ties with the callow Spencer/Coco/Whitney crowd, send her off to fortify her friendship with Sasha on page 277 (INCURABLE FLIRT).

This information is dynamite in Haley's hands. It's up to you to help her handle it in just the right way, before it all blows up in her face.

Just because a guy and a girl are sitting alone together, it doesn't mean they're flirting. Unless they're groping each other under the table.

Haley and Sasha rode to Bubbies bistro in Sasha's vintage Mustang at around eleven on Saturday night. Sasha parked right out front and the two girls went inside to pick up Johnny from work.

The dinner seating was over and the restaurant was pretty quiet, nearly empty, with most of the waiters and bus boys clearing the last of the tables and adding up tips.

"There he is," Sasha said, spotting Johnny in a back corner. She and Haley headed toward him, then

Haley suddenly stopped. Johnny wasn't alone at the table: sitting with him, just tucking into a late supper salad, was the big-haired beauty Mia Delgado.

"What's he doing with *her*?" Sasha gasped.

"I don't know," Haley said, but from the way he was leaning forward and the quiet, intimate way they were speaking, it didn't look good.

"Let's go find out," Sasha said, storming over to them. "Johnny, your ride's here."

Johnny looked up, startled. "Sasha—I didn't think you'd get here so early."

"I can see that," Sasha said.

"I'm all ready to go—I'll go finish up and get my tips." Johnny stood up and pushed through the swinging doors into the kitchen, untying his apron.

Mia smiled at Haley and Sasha. "Hello, girls. I love the food here, don't you?"

"It's grrreat," Sasha snarled.

Johnny returned a few minutes later. "Let's roll," he said. He gave Mia a little smile and a wave. "See you. Glad I could help with that . . . thing."

"Goodbye, Johnny. See you another time," Mia said. "Good luck with . . . you know." She winked at him. Haley could feel Sasha stiffen beside her.

Haley climbed into the backseat while Johnny rode shotgun and Sasha started the car. The tension between them made Haley nervous. She had a bad feeling she was about to witness another historic fight. She sometimes felt there should be Civil

War—type plaques posted around town to commemorate all of the famous Sasha-Johnny battles that had taken place.

"So?" Sasha said, pulling away from the curb. "Don't you have anything to say for yourself?"

"Sash, Mia is a Bubbies regular," Johnny said. "She flounces in with a different guy every night. Things were slow, I was finished with my shift, so I was just making small talk with her to pass the time."

Sasha rolled her eyes. "Small talk? Please. What was that little thing she said when we were leaving— 'Good luck with *you know*'? Good luck with *what*?"

"Nothing, Sash, I swear. You know how Mia is. Everything she says sounds like a come-on."

"So she was coming on to you, is that what you're saying?" Sasha was livid.

"Sasha, no!" Johnny said. "You've got to believe me. Haley, talk some sense into her, will you?"

● ● ●

What's Haley supposed to think? She keeps catching Mia in compromising situations. They can't all be innocent mistakes, can they?

If you are sure Mia is trouble and feel that Haley should warn Sasha that Mia has been flirting with Johnny since day one in Hillsdale, go to page 295 (JOHNNY BE GONE). If you'd rather Haley encourage Sasha to give Johnny the benefit of the doubt, go to page 299 (HAPPY ENDING). And if you believe Haley

should stay out of Sasha and Johnny's love life altogether, send her to focus on real drama on page 306 (THEATRICAL RELEASE). Finally, if you think Mia's asking for trouble and Whitney should know what she's been up to, send Haley to page 288 (HIGH SCHOOL HOME-WRECKER).

No man is safe with Mia around. Which means neither is any girl with a boyfriend, brother or father.

BASEMENT DWELLERS

What happens in the basement stays in the basement.

"The way you stood up to your parents was so cool, Irene," Haley said enthusiastically. "I mean it. My parents aren't half as strict as yours, but still, when it comes to certain issues they're touchy on, I sometimes chicken out."

Haley and Irene were lounging on the couch in Haley's basement, flipping through channels on the TV and working their way through a big bowl of popcorn. It was almost midnight on Saturday night and Haley's parents and Mitchell were in bed. Irene, at Haley's urging, had refused to obey her parents' wish that she quit working on the sets for the school play and spend more time at the Golden Dynasty instead. Haley thought Irene was such an incredible artist that she shouldn't let her talent go to waste, and Irene was beginning to believe in herself, too. Maybe, from now on, Irene's parents would start to see their daughter with new eyes as well.

"I'm still glad I'm sleeping over at your house tonight," Irene said. "Just in case . . . you know, they decide to backslide and chain me to the hostess station."

"Just let them try," Haley said. "Devon and Shaun and I will cut you free with a chain saw."

"Don't let Shaun near a chain saw," Irene said. "Ever." Haley laughed.

There was a tapping on the basement window. "Did you hear something?" Haley said.

"I bet it's the boys."

Haley went to the window and drew the curtain aside. Shaun's big blond face was pressed against the glass like a smashed pumpkin. Haley almost screamed, but caught herself just in time.

"Let us in!" Shaun said in a deep, creepy voice.

"Shhh!" Haley said. "Come around to the door." She opened the basement door and Shaun and Devon snuck in.

"Oh yea, poppers." Shaun dug his hand into the

bowl and stuffed his mouth with a fistful of popcorn. "Hales, you got any chocolate sauce?"

"Are you forgetting where you are?" Haley said. Her parents refused to keep anything sugary in the house. "I can get you wheatgrass juice or carrot shavings. Take your pick."

"Whatever." Shaun shrugged. "My stomach can take anything you throw at it."

"Be right back." Haley quietly went upstairs for some soda water and glasses and a few condiments for the boys. When she came back down she found Shaun on his hands and knees, bucking his legs and yelling, *"Hee-haaww! Heeee-haaawww!* Come on Irene, you up for a ride?"

Haley glanced at Devon, who looked nervous. Irene's eyes darted from one friend to another, embarrassed.

No way, Haley thought. She'd heard the rumors, but she didn't think they could really be true. Not even Shaun would take Method acting that far. . . .

But there he was, honking and bucking in his most donkey-brained fashion, even without the papier-mâché head.

● ● ●

Shaun certainly puts his whole heart—or ass—into everything he does, and he's apparently unembarrassable. The same can't be said of Irene, though—or Haley.

Maybe the creative types have gotten a little too freaky for Haley's taste.

If you think Haley should forget the theater crowd and focus on her upcoming academic challenges, send her to page 285 (TESTING LIMITS). If you believe Haley's loyalty, both to her friends and to the theater, will overcome any distaste for Shaun's antics, go to page 306 (THEATRICAL RELEASE).

Shaun has certainly been tamed a little by Irene, but will she keep him as her pet? Or will Mr. Chen impose a catch-and-release?

TESTING LIMITS

A mind is a terrible thing
to waste.

The moment of truth—or at least the first of many—
arrived. In the last five days the junior class brain
trust had taken the IQ test, the PSAT, the Myers-
Briggs Type Indicator . . . and they were utterly exhausted.

"I can't even speak I'm so fried," said Annie, fan-
ning herself with a notebook and putting her feet up
on the Metzgers' coffee table.

"My brain feels like the densely compressed center of a black hole," Dave babbled. "Or maybe a

freshly split nucleus." He continued with more spacy nonsense and then trailed off, stopping midsentence.

Annie had told Haley in confidence earlier that Mrs. Metzger was worried about Dave and had sent him to a psychiatrist for observation. However, after his earlier meltdown on the "Inside Hillsdale" videocasts, he now seemed to be acting fairly normal.

"Well, I feel great," Haley reported proudly. "I actually kind of liked taking the IQ test. It was sort of . . . fun."

Only Haley had managed to make it through this firestorm with her wits fully intact. After one good night of sleep, she'd recovered from the testing circuit, no sweat. "I think studying with Alex really helped me prepare mentally," she added. "I mean, he'd taken all these tests before and let me know exactly what to expect."

"I saw the chemical reaction happening between you two from the very beginning," mumbled Dave. "Like a gas burner meeting a highly flammable substance—puff. Ignited uncontrollably."

"There must be something you two do together besides study," Annie said, pressing for more details before a yawn got the best of her. For the first time since Haley had known her, Annie was actually too tired to interrogate her. Haley could tell by the exhausted look in Annie's eyes that what she really needed was a nap. Apparently, Dave did too. He'd just fallen asleep in his chair sitting up and was now snoring loudly.

"Okay, on that note . . . I'm going to give Alex a call and see if he wants to hang out. You people need to get some sleep."

Judging by the sparkle in Haley's eye as she shot up, it was obvious she was looking forward to seeing her senior "friend" again. She had already started dialing Alex's phone number as she walked toward the front door.

"See ya later, Annie," Haley said with a playful grin.

THE END

HIGH SCHOOL HOME-WRECKER

Sometimes models don't exhibit model behavior.

"Whitney, I've got something to tell you," Haley confided. She'd found Whitney in the cafeteria at lunchtime, scarfing down an ice cream sandwich. Upon hearing Haley's serious tone, Whitney glanced up nervously and said, "Just let me get some more ice cream first."

"In a minute," Haley said, sitting down beside Whitney. "After you hear what I have to say, even you might be too disgusted to eat."

"I doubt that," Whitney said. "Hit me."

"Remember how we were all wondering what Mia was doing at Mrs. Eton's Casino Night?" Haley said. Whitney nodded. "Well, I found out who invited her."

"Who?"

Haley swallowed. This was going to be hard. "It was your dad."

"My dad?" Whitney screeched. She paused for a moment to let this news sink in. Then she said, "I knew it! I knew something funny was going on between them. Did you see the way that slut was flirting with him at the party?" She jumped to her feet, forgetting about the second ice cream sandwich, and ran off.

"Where are you going?" Haley called after her.

"There's someone else who needs to know this," Whitney said. Haley's heart sank. This gossip bomb was clearly going to wipe out people for miles around.

Haley found out the next day that Whitney had cut English to run home and tell her stepmonster, Trish, that Jerry Klein was now cheating on her. How life does come full circle. Whitney had found Trish lying on the couch, watching soap opera reruns. Trish was of course upset by the news, and as soon as Jerry Klein got home from work that night, she let him have it. He denied everything—even knowing any Mia Delgado.

"You know that's not true," Haley told Whitney. "You saw him talking to her at the party. You saw it with your own eyes."

"You're right," Whitney said. "But I know Dad. He'll stick to his story unless someone confronts him with convertible proof."

"You mean incontrovertible proof," Haley said.

"That's what I said," Whitney replied.

"Well, I can get that for you." Haley made a call to Mrs. Eton's office, asking for the social secretary. All she had to do was say the secret code, "Garth," and the next thing she knew Rachel had faxed her a copy of Jerry Klein's guest list, which Haley gave to Whitney.

"This proves Dad's lying," Whitney told Trish when she showed her the fax. "Why would he spend $1,500 on a ticket for Mia if there wasn't something going on?" Within a week, Trish moved out of the house. Whitney had never been a big fan of hers, but she couldn't help feeling a little sorry for the former waitress.

Haley, meanwhile, felt sorry for Whitney, whose family was once again undergoing an upheaval thanks to her. Whitney was so stressed she started shoplifting and eating and repeating again. And all the while, Mia blithely went on in her usual flirtatious way, completely unfazed by the whole scandal. Nothing seemed to be able to shake that girl. She was truly shameless.

• • •

Haley's zeal to expose the ugly underbelly of Whitney's family didn't do anyone any good. The Kleins had always been dysfunctional; now they were basically destroyed. Whitney wasn't speaking to her dad, and her mom was so caught up in her new romance with Sasha's dad that she wasn't really there for Whitney either. *Kaboom.* All that progress Whitney had made these last few months, erased in a single afternoon.

If Haley was hoping to derail Mia's march through the male population of Hillsdale, that didn't work, either. Haley should have thought twice before setting off such a scandal bomb. Now it's too late.

You blew it. Go back to page 1.

CONCEALED WEAPON

If you're going to try to bury something, you'd better dig a really deep hole.

When Haley arrived at Whitney's house, she had already decided she was not going to tell anyone about Jerry Klein's alleged affair with Mia Delgado—especially not Whitney. But when Whitney invited her up to her bedroom and secretively closed the door behind them, Haley also realized she would probably need to confess if Whitney pressed her on the Mia subject.

"I wanted to ask you about something," Whitney began. "It's serious."

"Okay," Haley said, sitting down on Whitney's fluffy white bed, looking wide-eyed and innocent.

"Do you ever get really awful stomach pains that twist up your intestines into knots and make you want to bend over and cry?" she blurted out, gripping her waist.

"Do you mean *cramps*?" Haley asked, not sure where Whitney was going with this one, but relieved she wasn't talking about her dad and Mia Delgado.

"My stomach has been off for days," she went on.

"Maybe you should drink some herbal tea," Haley suggested. "I bet peppermint would settle your tummy. Is it stress? Everyone in our class seems to be succumbing to it lately."

Haley had hit the nail on the head. Whitney suddenly burst into tears.

"I can't believe I now live with Sasha's dad and that Sasha hasn't even come over once to visit me," she cried. "Not once. She has her own room here, right across the hall, and she doesn't even care. We used to be best friends! Do you know I designed my fall collection with her in mind?"

Haley put her arm around Whitney's shoulder. She was glad she had decided to butt out of the Kleins' ongoing scandals. Whitney had already been through enough upheaval in her family and seemingly couldn't stand much more.

"I know Sasha is going to come around, Whit. Maybe you should tell her how you're feeling."

"You think I should call her?" she whimpered, drying her tears with her sleeve.

"Yes, you should be the bigger person here and call. You'll feel better about it. I know you will."

"Thanks, Haley. Maybe I should. You're such a good friend. I don't know what I would do without you."

Haley smiled. She felt good about protecting her friend from all the rumors, and her conscience was crystal-clear.

"Here, I'll dial the number," she said, picking up Whitney's cell phone and looking forward to the day when she and Whitney and Sasha could all hang out as friends.

THE END

JOHNNY BE GONE

Don't jump to conclusions without a safety net.

"Hey, Haley—come with me." Sasha pulled up in front of Haley's house in her new car after school and rolled down the window. "Get in. We're going to see what Johnny's up to at work."

Haley hopped in and Sasha headed to Bubbies. Sasha had been going through a rough time with Johnny lately, and Haley figured she could use a supportive friend. Ever since she had caught Mia and Johnny cozying up to each other in a corner booth at the bistro, Sasha was convinced her boyfriend had a crush on *la modela*.

"I just can't stop thinking about it," Sasha muttered. "Mia. And Johnny. Together. Laughing, kissing, doing who knows what kind of exotic Spanish make-out techniques . . . Something's definitely going on. I just know it."

"Is Johnny expecting us?" Haley asked.

"No," Sasha said. "This way we can surprise him."

"Well, I wasn't going to tell you this, but Mia has been flirting with Johnny since the day she got here," Haley said. "You should see the way she hangs all over him in art class."

"Ugh!" Sasha hit the steering wheel with the palm of her hand. "Who does that Spanish bimbo think she is?"

"Someone should teach that girl a lesson," Haley said.

"I know just the person for the job," Sasha said. "Me."

The car skidded to a stop in front of the restaurant. Sasha stormed out, leaving Haley to follow in her wake. Sure enough, inside Johnny was sitting at the bar, talking intently with Mia.

"I don't mean to interrupt," Sasha said abruptly, disturbing the customers who were finishing their late lunches. "Mia, I'm surprised you even have time to hang out here, considering you're seducing my former best friend's father. And filming hookup sessions that air on the Internet. Is there any depth you won't sink to?"

Johnny reached out to calm Sasha down, but she brushed him away. "You haven't heard her side," he said.

"Oh, and I suppose you have? That's what's going on here? She's crying on your shoulder? You're a greedy little slut who can't keep her hands off any man who walks by!" She stabbed a finger in Mia's face. "Why don't you go back to Spain and stick to what you're good at; topless modeling?"

Haley saw wrath flicker across Mia's face. But Mia was nothing if not an excellent actress. She glanced sideways at Johnny, and within seconds, her eyes were welling up with tears. Johnny reached over and tenderly put a hand on her shoulder.

"Clearly, you've made your choice, I hope you don't mind sharing her with half of Hillsdale," Sasha said, stomping out of the restaurant, ignoring the whispers and stares of the stunned customers. Haley followed her dutifully and got back into the car.

"That'll show them," Sasha muttered.

"You had to do it," Haley said. "You can't let people get away with sneaking around behind your back."

"Then how come I feel so terrible?" Sasha asked. Unlike Mia's, her tears were real.

· · ·

Now Sasha needs a shoulder to cry on. But maybe Haley's wouldn't be the best choice? She's the one who urged Sasha to make a scene.

A few days later, Sasha found out that Johnny and Mia weren't fooling around behind her back at all; in fact, Johnny had been asking Mia's advice about a piece of jewelry he wanted to buy for Sasha to celebrate their one-year anniversary. Needless to say, he never bought that necklace. Sasha didn't have the nerve to beg him to take her back, but he wouldn't have done it anyway— not after the way she'd humiliated them all at Bubbies.

Sasha's just made a huge mistake, and Haley was the only one who could have talked her out of it. Let's hope Haley can do better next time, now that she's learned her lesson.

Go back to page 1.

HAPPY ENDING

It's easy to be happy when things are going your way.

"I can't believe you actually thought there was something going on between me and Mia," Johnny said to Sasha, practically laughing.

Haley had gone to Bubbies with Sasha as backup, to confront Johnny and try to clear things up between them. There Haley was, standing awkwardly in the middle of their conversation and feeling like an intruder in their private affairs.

"I didn't really think so," Sasha said. "But when I saw you two together I just . . . wondered. It seemed like you two were confiding in each other. And I'm still not convinced she's the most trustworthy girl."

"Well, we were keeping a secret," Johnny announced. Haley braced herself. "This." He took from his pocket a small blue box tied with a white ribbon and gave it to Sasha. "Go ahead, open it."

Sasha looked confused, but her face softened completely once she opened the box. Inside was a gold sunburst medallion hanging from a delicate chain. Engraved on the back of the medallion were the words *Sasha + Johnny. Year one.*

"Johnny," Sasha gasped.

"I was going to give it to you on our anniversary."

"It's beautiful."

Sensing Johnny's sideways glances in her direction, Haley took two steps backward and pulled out her cell phone, trying to figure out someone to text-message. She realized she definitely needed to let them have their moment.

"I thought that since Mia was a model, she might know some cool new designer that you would love," Johnny explained. "She sent me to a store in the city, and I found this."

"I love it!" Sasha put the necklace on. "But it looks really expensive." She seemed concerned with how he had afforded such an extravagant gift.

"Why do you think I've been working here at Bubbies?" Johnny said. "Though it turns out, the tips are better than you'd expect. I might actually keep this job."

Sasha hugged him tight. "I'm sorry I ever doubted you," she whispered, nuzzling his neck.

As Haley stood there watching Sasha and Johnny make out, she suddenly realized her own life needed tending to. She pulled up an old text from Reese on her phone. It read, "Sorry I had to cancel dinner. Make it up to you soon. Promise." Haley frowned. "Soon" never seemed to arrive. Haley walked toward the bathroom, tears rolling down her cheeks. She was feeling sorry for herself that she didn't have a boyfriend who was out buying her jewelry. In the mirror, she silently promised herself she would confront the Reese situation. She adored him, but she couldn't go on like this, never seeing him and always coming second—make that fifth, behind soccer, family, friends and his all-important GPA.

Perhaps it was time to move on.

THE END

WATCH AND LEARN

People can sometimes teach you more than schoolbooks.

Haley and Reese had both had a grueling week of testing, homework and soccer matches, so she fully expected him to bail on weekend plans. But much to Haley's surprise, Reese asked her to go to the school play, *A Midsummer Night's Dream* on Friday night. It was a thrill to be sitting alone in the dark with Reese once again. Even though he'd been preoccupied lately, Haley still had strong feelings for him.

"Shaun's hilarious," Haley whispered. It was the

scene in which Shaun Willkommen, as the weaver Nick Bottom, wakes up from a dream with an ass's head instead of a man's.

"A comedian is born," Reese whispered back. The audience roared while Shaun ran around the stage on all fours and kicked up his back legs donkey-style. Reese, too, was laughing out loud.

At first, when Reese had come over to her house that evening to pick her up, Haley saw the tension in his face from all the recent stress. But now, as Haley watched him laughing, Reese looked transformed, as if he didn't have a care in the world. He smiled at Haley and put his arm around her. She snuggled in close. What a relief it was to finally have his full attention.

After the play ended and the audience cheered and called out "Bravo! Bravo!" Reese and Haley migrated outside with the masses.

"Your sets were gorgeous," Haley said to Irene, who slipped out from a stage door.

"Thanks," Irene mumbled, sheepishly. Haley noticed she seemed glad to have her work acknowledged.

"What do you say we stop for ice cream," Reese suggested after he and Haley had congratulated the cast. "If you're lucky I might even let you get your favorite—mint chip with chocolate sprinkles."

Haley was impressed he remembered her favorite

flavor. But before she could answer him, Reese took her in his arms and kissed her. It was the perfect kind of kiss too: the cozy boyfriend kiss. And it went on . . . and on . . . and on.

"I owe you an apology," Reese said, touching his forehead to hers and looking deep into her eyes. "I'm sorry I've been so distracted lately. I know I haven't been a good boyfriend. It's just that . . . I'm starting to get serious about college. Which doesn't mean I'm not serious about you. It's just a lot to balance is all, and I haven't been doing a very good job of it."

"I understand," Haley said. She knew the Highlands had soaring expectations for their only son. He was so good at so many things he tried, it had gotten to a point where he wasn't allowed to be less than perfect. At anything. "We're all under a lot of pressure," Haley said. "Some of us have parents who are pushing us and some of us put that pressure on ourselves, but we're all feeling it. Believe me."

Just then, they heard tires screech by on asphalt. "Need a ride, lovers?" someone yelled from Spencer's sports car. Haley recognized Coco, Mia and Whitney as his passengers.

"Not a chance," Reese replied long after they'd blown by. "I can't believe I used to be friends with those kids. So how about that ice cream?"

Right at that moment Haley knew she was exactly where she was supposed to be, with the only guy who mattered: her beloved Reese. He wrapped his arm around Haley as they strolled toward the ice cream shop. Haley sighed, utterly content. It was good to have the old Reese back again.

THE END

THEATRICAL RELEASE

Performance anxiety comes in many forms.

It was opening night of the big Hillsdale production of *A Midsummer Night's Dream*. Haley had rehearsed her lines until she knew them in her sleep, but she was still terrified of forgetting something crucial. The dressing room buzzed with excitement as Whitney hopped from actor to actor with pins between her teeth, double-checking every costume and making sure every piece of flair was intact, just as she'd intended.

"Opening night!" Irene said enthusiastically as she zipped Haley into her costume. "Nervous?"

"No," Haley lied. "Why should I be nervous? I am Helena."

Irene laughed. "Please. Save the lines for your audience. Even I'm nervous, and I don't have to set foot onstage."

Shaun was pacing the room, muttering to himself, "I am the ass, forsooth I am the ass. . . ."

Haley realized that everyone around her was probably feeling the same jitters she was. To settle herself down, she headed over to hair and makeup.

Once her face and coif were done, Haley stood with Irene in the wings, counting down the minutes to curtain.

"Take a peek," suggested Irene. Haley parted the curtain just a crack and gazed out at the audience. She was blown away by the crowd. But even more impressive was Irene's set design.

"Irene, the forest looks spectacular," Haley said, genuinely awestruck. "It *is* the magical forest where the fairies live." Haley's stomach lurched as she caught a glimpse of her parents, Mitchell, her teachers and all her friends sitting in the first few rows. She quickly pulled the curtain shut, feeling slightly panicked. "Maybe peeking isn't such a good idea."

Irene patted her on the shoulder. "Don't sweat it. You're really talented. The audience is going to love you. What am I saying? They already do. I think I saw your Gam Polly out there."

"Really?" Haley asked, excited.

"You're so lucky, Irene. Your work is already done."

"You think so?" Irene challenged. "Try moving those giant sets around without knocking one over. We'll be lucky if we don't conk somebody on the head with a tree by the end of the night."

"Places, everybody!" Assistant Director Coco shouted, clapping her hands authoritatively.

"Man, that girl sure loves bossing people around," Irene whispered. "I'd better go. Break a leg!"

"Thanks!" Haley took her place backstage among her fellow actors. The curtain went up, and the play began.

When she heard her cue and stepped onstage, the lights dazzled her for a moment, but then she recovered her composure. Her lines poured out of her as naturally as if she were speaking them for the first time. She forgot herself and really did become Helena, the lovelorn maiden. When the moment came for Demetrius, played by Devon, to suddenly realize he's loved Helena all along, Haley felt as if she and Devon were the only people on the planet, living through this beautiful moment. His eyes shone, and he kissed her with real emotion.

Mia drew cheers for her portrayal of Titania, and Spencer somehow pulled off a puckish Puck in spite of having blown off the last dress rehearsal. But it was Shaun's portrayal of Nick Bottom that brought down the house.

When the play was over, the entire cast received a standing ovation. As the final curtain fell, they jumped up and hugged each other, laughing. Haley never knew being in a play could be so thrilling.

As Haley went back to the dressing room, which buzzed with talk of an afterparty, Xavier Willkommen breezed in to find his four pupils.

"There you are, my starth!" he cried, wiping away a tear. "You were brilliant, BRILLIANT, all of you! Thhaun, it lookth like you've inherited the family acting gene!"

Irene and Haley exchanged a quick glance and tried not to laugh. Xavier was an awesome teacher, but his acting was less than spectacular. Shaun, however, had proved that you could make anything happen as long as you had enough passion.

Joan and Perry and Mitchell came in to congratulate Haley, beaming with pride. They were trailed closely by Gam Polly.

"My girl," Gam said proudly.

"You were *really* good," Mitchell, dressed primly in his tiny blazer and bow tie, said. "Here, these are for you."

He handed her an armful of yellow roses. Haley breathed in their sweet scent and smiled brightly.

"Thanks, you guys," she said. "And thanks, Mitchell, for not taking the roses apart before giving them to me."

"I wouldn't do that, silly," Mitchell said. "You can't put flowers back together again."

Standing there with her family, friends and fellow cast members, the adrenaline still coursing through her veins, Haley knew she would always remember this night. She felt deeply satisfied knowing she'd taken a chance on performing in the school play. Even though her part was a supporting one. She came out feeling like a star. And on top of all that, she had Devon, her leading man.

THE END

LIZ RUCKDESCHEL was raised in Hillsdale, New Jersey, where *What if . . .* is set. She graduated from Brown University with a degree in religious studies and worked in set design in the film industry before turning her attention toward writing. Liz currently lives in Los Angeles.

SARA JAMES has been an editor at *Men's Vogue*, covered the media for *Women's Wear Daily*, been a special projects producer for *The Charlie Rose Show*, and written about fashion for *InStyle* magazine. Sara graduated from the University of North Carolina at Chapel Hill with a degree in English literature. She grew up in Cape Hatteras, North Carolina, where her parents have owned a surf shop since 1973.